Forty Days of Tucker J.

Stretching out in bed one late September morning, a broad grin spreads over Tucker Jenkins' face. His school days are over, finished for good. From now on, his time is his own.

But Tucker's newly-found freedom is short-lived. With one in three school leavers out of work, Tucker's Dad wants to see his son get some more qualifications to improve his chances of getting a job. He issues an ultimatum: Tucker has until half-term – just forty days – to find means of earning some money, otherwise it's back to school for him.

Learning to live on the dole is an education all of its own, but as Tucker takes his place in the queues at the Employment Office and Job Centre, he's determined never to have to walk back through the gates of Grange Hill again.

ROBERT LEESON

Forty Days
of Tucker J.

Based on the BBC television series
TUCKER'S LUCK
by Phil Redmond

FONTANA LIONS

First published in Fontana Lions 1983
by William Collins Sons & Co Ltd
14 St James's Place, London SW1X 3LA

Printed in Great Britain
by William Collins Sons & Co Ltd, Glasgow

Day One

At 09.45 hours Tucker Jenkins woke.

One hairy muscular leg sticking out from the side of the duvet gave a twitch. And at the other corner, where a tangle of hair showed above the bedclothes, an eye opened. Then a bare arm struggled out into the open, bent at the elbow and turned the watch on the wrist towards the eye.

Quarter to ten. He was late for school.

No he wasn't. It was summer holidays.

No it wasn't, it was September 6.

He was late for school.

No he wasn't, he'd left.

These thoughts banged into the rear of each other in his mind like cars in an M-1 pile up, all in a split second. His body jerked as he tried to respond to each thought in turn. Then he lay back, stretched and his other eye came open. The rest of his face pulled free from the edge of the duvet and a broad grin spread over it.

He'd left. He'd finished. He wasn't going back, ever again. From now on, his time was his own.

He looked across the edge of the bed-clothes at the room, lit up by the autumn sun which had struggled through the steamed up windows. His eye picked up a trail of clothing, jeans on the floor, shirt with a tie still round the collar (why was he wearing a tie last night?) over the back of the chair, together with the wiring harness from his bike, like a greasy snake in its grubby rubber covering and then the jacket on the table.

He raised his head an inch. It felt as though the back was coming off it. (What had he been doing last night? What

5

was the good of enjoying your freedom if you couldn't remember what you were doing with it?)

He sank back. Suddenly his whole body felt heavy again. His eye lids were closing. He could feel them moving down his eyeballs. He was going off to sleep again. He couldn't wake up.

Vaguely he recalled that bloke Sutcliffe had been reading about in an English lesson – Russian geezer, who wouldn't get out of bed. Must have been in the old days. Sutcliffe reckoned he was making a protest about life. That was it. His eyes closed again.

At 11.00 hours when the world had moved round a notch, the sun shone through the window again, right into Tucker's eyes. Not a bad aim from 93 million miles. He grunted, swallowed. His mouth tasted foul. He ought to get up and have some coffee. And decide what to do. He looked across the room to the armchair where a spare carburettor sat on a spread out newspaper.

There was his bike to fix. Then he remembered. He needed a new set of contact breakers. And that would not leave much change out of five quid. Did he have five quid? No he didn't. He had . . .? Reaching out a long arm he tried to pull his jeans from the back of the chair to reach his pockets. The jeans, caught in the wiring harness stayed put. A jerk and they came free as chair, harness and all toppled over. Inside the pocket were a few coins. He felt them. No more than 75p.

Lying back and resting his fragile head, he let his gaze move round the room while he considered his next move. On the centre of the wall, between two bike mag pull-outs was the design he'd done for the school magazine. His prize-winning design. He'd bought a Premium Bond for the money. Now if that came up this weekend – say £100,000, he could buy a set of points and have £99,996.50p change. And if he invested that at—what? eight per cent? – he'd have . . . Then he stopped; this was more brain beating than going back to school.

12.30 hours: He was awake again. The sun had given up and had moved round to the other side of the house. Then he noticed something on the table. Something blue. Struggling up in bed, he stared again.

It was a five pound note. His mother must have left it for him. It was Monday. He leapt out of bed, tripped over the wiring harness and banged his head on the table. But it didn't even hurt him. There were two five pound notes. A ten. This must be the new system.

Pulling on his jeans, he wandered into the bathroom. His head had stopped throbbing. Splashing water on his face, he ran his fingers through his hair and nodded amiably to the face in the mirror. Back in the passage outside he paused a moment in thought, then taking the stairs in three strides, he picked up the phone, and dialled. After a dozen rings, a voice answered.

'Yeah.'

'Alan. Get up.'

'I am up'

'Well why are you holding the phone under the bed clothes, then?'

'Ha—ha'

'When you're up, I'll buy you a 'burger. This bloke on the radio, Madness Pipe, says it's a complete meal with a bit of lettuce.'

'Can't, Tucker. I'm going to college.'

'Listen, Alan. Stay where you are. I'll get an ambulance. You can get treatment for that.'

'Leave it. Susi's going down for registration. I'm going with her – and have a look round, could be interesting.'

'Could be lethal. Registration, mate. You're out of your box. We finished with all that.'

'Listen, Tucker. See you. Got to rush.'

13.00 hours: The bike shop was closed for the afternoon. That was just as well. Tommy was in the caff, though. Tucker and he settled down for a civilised afternoon.

15.00 hours: They moved on to the club.

Tucker won three quid off Tommy at pool then generously played on so that Tommy won two back. By this time, the sun had packed in and gone home. The club was closed but other places were open. Tommy and Tucker moved on.

21.00 hours: At ease in the pub Tucker and Tommy became aware that they were being watched. Across the other side of the bar, in the lounge were two girls. One, taller than the other had an impudent glance. When Tucker's eye caught hers she stared back with friendly challenge in her look.

21.30 hours. 'Let's move round there,' suggested Tommy. Tucker shrugged. Tommy was always in a hurry. 'O.K.', he agreed at last. On the way round the bar, it occured to Tucker to nip smartly into the gents. A minute later, Tommy burst in and lined up next to Tucker. He laughed breathlessly.

'I was just going to sit down when these two blokes arrived. They'd been there all the time, but they'd been chatting up the barmaid.'

'What, did they see you?' asked Tucker, throwing a quick glance over his shoulder.

'Nah. They were too thick for that. Herberts like them deserve all they get.'

'You want to watch it, Tommy. You're too quick off the mark.'

'All right Dad. Come on I'll buy you another.'

'What with?'

'All right. You'll buy me another.'

01.00 hours: Tucker made his way carefully up the stairs to his own front door. To his surprise, the light was on in the kitchen. To his even greater surprise, the door opened just as he was fiddling his key into the lock.

To his still greater surprise, his Dad stood in the doorway.

'There you are,' said Mr Jenkins. There was no answer to that. In any case Tucker said nothing. He had the feeling Day Two was starting too early.

Day Two

Mr Jenkins closed the door behind Tucker. He looked round the kitchen. His mother sat at the table.

'Cup of tea, Peter?'

Tucker stared. What were they doing up at this time – both fully dressed? Something was happening and he couldn't make out what it was. His head seemed to revolve gently round on his shoulders. He sat down quickly and grinned.

'Ta, Mum. What are you two doing up at this time? It's bad for you, you know.'

His mother's lips drew together. Her eyes looked past him at his father, who was locking the door. She was giving Tucker some message, but what it was he couldn't work out. He took the cup of tea she poured out and drank. Would you believe it, he was thirsty.

His Dad sat down.

'I've been trying to have a word with you for the past three nights,' he began.

Tucker started to say something witty about making an appointment when he caught his Dad's glance and decided to say nothing. In any case, Mr Jenkins was not making conversation.

'We've been having a word . . .'

Oh, they had, had they?

'About your future, since you don't seem to be thinking about it yourself . . .'

'Hey, I'm looking for a job.'

'Oh yes? And where did you look for one today?'

'Well, here and there.'

'Pull the other one. You haven't even been to see about signing on, have you?' His father's voice was calm, but it wasn't friendly.

Tucker thought quickly.

'They don't let you sign on before the school holidays end.' he said. Lucky he'd remembered that.

'You mean they don't start paying you before the end of the holidays. There's nothing to stop you signing on, or looking for a job. And to be honest, your performance so far doesn't show much interest, either . . .'

His father paused, then suddenly asked, 'How much have you got left of that ten quid?'

'What ten quid?' Tucker asked, before he could stop himself. Now his father was narked, he could see that.

'That ten quid is to see you through the week – your mid-day meals and anything else, clothes, and any other extras.'

'Eh?'

Jenkins senior's face began to change colour. Tucker's Mum put a hand on his arm. Her eyes signalled, 'Peter!'

Then Tucker's Dad changed his tack. 'Look. Let's look at it straight. I don't think you're going to get a job in a month of Sundays.' He jerked a thumb over his shoulder. 'They reckon one in three school leavers stand a chance of getting a job, a real job I mean, not one of these Mickey Mouse training things. And the ones who get the jobs are the ones with qualifications. What have you got?'

'I,' began Tucker. But his Dad wasn't really asking him. He ploughed on.

'We've been in to school this evening and had a word. There's a one year Technical Engineering Course at the college. But you need your maths for that. Now they're doing crash courses in the sixth form. If you went back, you could walk it. You're intelligent enough. They know it. So do I. But you'll have to work.'

Tucker stared, mouth open.

Then he said, slowly, 'Go—back—to—school. You . . .'

Then he stopped himself just in time and drank quickly from his cup. He felt his mouth fill with tea leaves. He swallowed and then said calmly, looking his father in the eye.

'Well, I'm not. I am not going back to school. I've had enough. I'm signing on and I'm getting a job, one way or another.'

There was a silence. Tucker's mother glanced quickly at his father, then filled his cup. But Tucker's Dad was suddenly quite calm.

'O.K.,' he said. 'I think you ought to go back to school. It's free until you're nineteen. After nineteen we have to pay. I think you ought to get more education. You don't. So go ahead. Get yourself a job.'

A weight rose up from Tucker's mind, then sank down again as his Dad went on.

'But you're on your own. When you get your dole money, you keep ten quid back, that's your lot. The rest goes to your Mum. You want to play at being one of the Unemployed, well play the game by the rules and see how you go.'

Mr Jenkins paused.

'I still think you're going back to school. They told me they'll keep a place for you up to half term. I've to let them know by October 15. So I'll make a bargain with you. You

11

get yourself a permanent job – O.K. Or even get yourself casual work. They let you earn four quid a week on top of your dole, don't they? You earn, say, £25 by that time – O.K., you can carry on. Otherwise, you're going back to school.'

Tucker's Mum looked at him.

'Another cup of tea, Peter?'

'No thanks.'

When Tucker woke up it was mid-afternoon. He dressed and staggered round to the caff for a cup of coffee. He couldn't face any more. There was no sign of Tommy or Alan. Tommy was probably having it away merrily somewhere, though knowing Alan, he'd probably be having a miserable time with Susi and loving it.

He drifted along to the shopping precinct and looked in the Job Centre window. On the display board, several cards promised him executive status and the chance to earn up to £20,000 a year, if he was thirty, presentable and had a car. Reluctantly he tried the door. But is was shut for the afternoon.

Back home he slumped on to the settee and glowered at the box. They were showing a series about life in some school. He hadn't the strength to switch off and was still watching it when his Mum and Tracy came in.

"Hey Mum, look. Our Peter's watching children's television."

After tea, he retired to his room and sat down on the bed. He was too pre-occupied to notice that his Mum had been round the room. All the parts for his bike had been dumped together in a box in the corner and his clothes had been put away.

Emptying his pockets he found three pounds and some coins. He went out to the cinema, on his own. It was a horror movie, but even that couldn't raise his spirits.

He went back home and sat on the bed again. The calendar on the wall told him it was September 7. What had his Dad said? October 15. That meant he had—how long? He counted up. Thirty-eight days.

Ah well, today was a write-off anyway. He got up to get undressed then stopped. As well as putting clothes away, somebody had been shifting things on the cupboard top by his bed. He looked closely, then picked up the alarm clock. Someone had set it for half past seven in the morning. What a liberty.

He switched it off, then put out the light and went to bed.

Day Three

Tucker was dreaming. He had won a quarter of a million with his Premium Bond and his bank manager was advising him how to invest it. He sat at ease in an arm chair while the bank manager crouched in front of him humbly.

'Building Society investment now?' suggested the bank manager, 'that's nice and steady at 7.75 per cent.'

'Boring,' answered Tucker and gently kicked the bank manager.

'Government stock, 8¾, convertible to 9 per cent in 1985?' the gentleman wheedled from his position on the carpet.

'They've got enough of their own money, they're not having mine.' Tucker pushed the manager away from his foot which that worthy was trying to embrace.

'Aerodynamics are going up. Shipping's going down. Goldfield's high yield...' The manager, hands clasped together rose up to Tucker's side. 'Computers, very sound, replace people, people quite unreliable...'

13

Tucker yawned. The manager fearful of losing his attention, grasped him by the shoulder and pleadingly shook it. Tucker brushed him away. The shaking became harder.

Tucker was wide awake, sitting up in bed. His Dad stood by the bedside.

'I set your alarm for half seven. Didn't go off for some reason. Up you get.'

'Get up? What for?'

'You know what for. Signing on. You didn't do it yesterday, did you?'

Tucker yawned again, scratched himself and struggled from the bed. By half past eight, he had washed, dressed, breakfasted and was alone in the house.

Half past eight. What was he going to do? Nowhere would be open now. Not if they were in their right minds.

He thought for a bit. Well, he'd been got out of bed. There was nothing for it. Somebody else had to suffer. He went to the phone and dialled Alan's number.

By half past nine, he had assembled Alan, looking puffy-eyed and sleepy and Tommy, looking mutinous, in the precinct.

'What's all this for?' demanded Tommy. 'I'd only just got into bed.'

'We're signing on, that's what. We're going to the Labour.'

'You don't go to the Labour – that's for when you're out of work. You go to the Job Centre.'

'Nah. That's for when you want to be out of work. I tell you it's the Labour Exchange.'

'They don't call it the Labour Exchange, they call it the Employment Office.'

'Right, then, same difference. Let's go down and collect our money.'

'I'm having a coffee first,' said Alan, suddenly becoming belligerent. 'And what's more you are paying. This was your stupid idea.'

At half past ten the trio walked into the Employment Office. It had once been a church and it still had a solemn air about it. Queues of people, young and old, men and women, slowly wound their way across the large hall under its high roof towards a long counter. Behind the counter, under large notices suspended by chains from the ceiling, labelled 'Box 6', 'Box 7', right along to 'Box 14', sat the clerks, like priests waiting to bless the faithful.

'Hey, where do we go?' asked Tommy.

Tucker shrugged: 'Where d'you think. Shortest queue.'

'Maybe they're alphabetical,' said Tommy.

'If they are,' answered Alan, 'then I'm first. Humphreys, Jenkins, Watson.' He stepped forward pushing Tucker to one side. A slight push and shove developed which flowed over into the next queue. A large, bad tempered bloke in overalls told them to shove off, or words to that effect. They grinned at each other and settled down.

Half an hour later, Alan reached the counter at Box 6, with Tucker and Tommy behind him. The clerk behind the desk was a young lady, neat in blouse and jacket, her hair pinned back firmly.

'We want to sign on for the dole,' said Alan.

She looked up at him and held out her hand.

'Your P-45 please?'

'P-45?'

'Yes,' said the girl patiently. Then she raised her eyebrows. 'Didn't you get your P-45 when you left?'

'Left where?' Alan was getting bewildered.

'Your job.'

'We haven't had a job.'

'Well, you can't claim unemployment benefit then.' She looked them over, pursed her lips and then raising her voice so that several people nearby turned round: 'Are you school leavers?'

Alan nodded.

'Then go down to Box 13 and see Mr Hughes. Next please.'

Mr Hughes at Box 13, was middle-aged, fat and jovial. He grinned at them. 'Yes, gents.'

Tucker took charge.

'We want to sign on for benefit. Do we get that here?'

'No, squire. You don't get your benefit here.'

Tucker was about to boil over, when Box 13 went on. 'But if you don't come here, you don't get it, if you see what I mean. You want the Job Centre.'

'I don't get it, what's the difference between this place and the Job Centre, then?'

'Well, the Job Centre has a carpet for one thing,' replied the clerk with unfailing good humour. Tucker began to feel like strangling him. Maybe the snooty lady at Box Six would be better.

'Job Centres do jobs mainly. We do unemployment benefit. Some exchanges do both. It's all intended to confuse you and keep you occupied, squire. The thing is that you, as a school leaver, are a New Claim, and new claims go to the Job Centre.'

He looked at Tucker and read his thoughts. 'I am sorry, son, I did not invent the system. I only work it. Anyway, you go to the Job Centre. When you're fixed up, you'll be coming here – at least till you get a job, which, believe it or not, I hope will be very soon.'

By 12 o'clock they were back at the Job Centre filling in forms.

'Now, take this to the Social Security Office in High-field,' said the clerk.

'We don't want social security.'

'You do, you know. Look, unemployment benefit you

16

don't get until you've worked twenty-six weeks. While you're waiting for that happy day, you get Supplementary Benefit.'

'How much do we get?'

'When you take your form to the Social Security, they'll tell you. But if you like, get your NI 196, or is it the SB1, I can't remember, from the Post Office and that'll tell you. It all depends on your circumstances.'

When they got to Highfield, the Social Security Office was closed for lunch. They trailed back to the Arndale and rested their feet over a beefburger. At two o'clock, Tucker got up.

'Come on. Let's get this done.'

But now the troops mutinied. Alan and Tommy refused to walk a step further. Tucker looked at them.

'You're useless, that's what you are,' he said, and left them sitting over their empty coffee cups and strips of wilted lettuce. He pressed on to the Social Security office.

After an hour's wait, he was granted an interview. He was cross-questioned about his family.

'Well, there's me Mum . . .'

'No, have you any children?'

He was about to answer, 'None to speak of,' when he judged the time was not ripe for humour and simply answered yes or no.

Was he living apart from his parents? Did he have more than £2,000 in savings? Did he have unearned income? The questions went on. Suddenly Tucker began to feel guilty, then he felt angry, then he felt resigned. He just wanted to get the business over and get away.

'Take this form to the Employment Office.'

'Not the Job Centre?'

'No, not the Job Centre this time, the Employment Office.'

He made it to the Employment Office just before they

17

closed at four o'clock. They gave him his attendance card and told him to come back on Friday to sign on.

'You'll be Box Six,' said the clerk.

'Ah, the girl of my dreams,' answered Tucker.

'I beg your pardon.'

'Nothing.'

'Now take this form back to the Social Security.'

'I don't believe it.'

'I'm afraid you'll have to. Come back to us on Friday. The sooner you get it done, the sooner we can pay you your money. And don't forget, call in at the Job Centre every day if you can, and you being a school leaver, you ought to go to the Careers Office.'

'What's the difference between a career and a job.'

'Search me, squire, you'll find out when you get there.' The clerk grinned at Tucker. 'Good luck.'

The Job Centre was closed when he got round there. The Careers Office was never open on Wednesdays, but they stayed open till 7p.m. on Tuesdays. Big help. Tucker went home.

As he crawled into the living room, they were watching the end of the news on television.

The announcer said:

'Today the Stock Exchange share index was up seven points at 632.5.'

Tucker mouthed at the figure on the screen.

'What was that you said, Peter?' his mother sounded shocked.

'Nothing.' said Tucker.

Day Four

The alarm woke Tucker at half past seven. He lashed out and sent it spinning to the floor. His Dad must have nipped in and set it last night when he was watching the box.

But he was awake. He found himself getting up and dressing as if he did this every day of his life, like a zombie. Was this how it would be from now on? He put that thought on one side immediately and went to get his breakfast.

His Dad looked up from the table as much as to ask, 'Well, did you?' Before the words could come out, he said aggressively: 'Yes I did.' That closed the conversation and the rest of breakfast passed in silence.

There was no answer from Alan's phone, and when he called at Tommy's ten minutes later, there was no answer there. Now either they were still asleep or they were up early trying to work their way through the system. He thought for a moment whether he should look for them and offer his expert advice, but on second thoughts decided to get on with the next move in his life. It was like the kid's game, snakes and ladders, up one, back down again, go back two moves, wait, miss a turn – go forward two places.

He stopped in front of the Job Centre in the precinct. He'd often noticed it in its grubby orange and white trim and never given it a second thought. Now he had to go in there.

The notice on the door *No Dogs Please* gave him a brief laugh and then he took a breath and walked in. It was warm after the autumn air outside. It was dead quiet. It was empty save for a man in a dark suit at the reception desk who did not even look up from his paper work.

As he turned to the first board, with its rows of cards with their faint lines of typing he realised he had nothing to make notes on.

He turned to the reception desk. The man did not raise his head. Tucker coughed. Without a word, the man picked up a blank sheet of paper from the side and held it out. Tucker went back to the board. Suddenly he found himself becoming mildly excited.

'Sales Rep. £7000 a year, company car and expenses.' Hm, not bad. Then he read the bottom line – '25 plus.'

'Insurance rep – 24-30.'

'Life underwriter, 25-45, rigid.' What the hell did that mean?

'Car salesman, 23-plus.'

Ah. 'Trainee sales rep, £85 p.w.' No – 24-plus.

He moved away from 'Sales.'

'Alarm Service Engineer, 23-40; Typewriter Engineer, 25-30 fully experienced; Guage grinder, 30-plus; brick-layer, 40-plus; stove enamel sprayer, five years' experience; joiner, 40-plus; caretaker, 40-plus.'

He moved on. He wasn't making notes any more.

'Good speaking voice, £200 p.w.' Why not? Over 25, that's why.

'Up to £195 a week, no experience.' That was him – but 19-25.

'Fit, trustworthy' – and 30-55 as well.

At last he found: 'Clerk-typist, 18-plus.' Maybe he could fiddle that. Then he read: 'Must have experience.' And did he really want to be a clerk typist? Was he that desperate?

He moved on. He was at the last board: 'Train in confectionery.' ??? Why not. 18-plus? Why not? 'Start work at 5.30 a.m. and occasional nights.'

'Part time assistant.' No experience. No age given. He was about to turn to the reception desk, when he noticed 'Suit early retired person.' He wasn't that – yet.

'Hotel porter, £65-70, 18-25, 8-5p.m. or 2-11p.m.' Was that him?

No, they could have his days. They weren't having his nights as well.

'Cashier. Must be fit' He stared. What was that for? In case they sent the boys round? He turned abruptly and walked to the desk, remembering in time to note the reference number on the card.

The man looked up, looked as though he was going to shake his head, then picked up the phone and dialled a number. Two minutes later he put it down again.

'Sorry. That one's gone. We'll have to take the card out.' He smiled. 'It's always happening. Still keep looking.' He paused, 'Have you tried the Careers Centre?'

Tucker went back to the board. There were two cards left. The jobs had no age or experience bar on them. They were 'part time cook' and 'cleaner dish washer.'

Tucker walked out and strolled round to the Careers Office. The Careers Officer was out, but his secretary booked Tucker in to see him on Friday.

It was lunch time. At the caff he tried a fishburger for a change. Life stretched away in front of him – hamburger, cheeseburger, fishburger, beefburger. No sign of Alan and Tommy. He went home.

He lay on his bed, slowly turning the pages of the booklet he'd picked up in the Careers Office. It was all about being positive on the dole. The thing was, they said, to get a routine:

'Do the housework, call at the Job Centre, go swimming, read the adverts in the papers at the library, take the dog for a walk, dig the allotment, go to the youth club, water your pot plants, sign on, read a book, take a course in needlework, welding, playing the violin, brew parsnip wine, sign on, go swimming, read the adverts.'

He threw it across the room.

He was down to his last £1.50. When did that bloody giro cheque come?

Day Five

Tucker had hidden the alarm, but he woke up at seven o'clock anyway and couldn't get back to sleep.

At a quarter past nine he was at the Job Centre.

"You can meet old friends there," that stupid leaflet said. They were right, the old friends were the job cards he'd looked at yesterday. They'd even forgotten to remove the one about the fit cashier.

He walked out and headed for the Employment Office. And there he did meet an old friend. As he headed for the entrance he heard an Irish voice, loud and good humoured, from the edge of the pavement. It was Paddy Riordan, who'd worked with Tucker's brother on the site behind their flats. He was handing out leaflets. Paddy never gave up, did he?

Tucker moved on into the Exchange. The queue at Box 6 was longish, but not too long. He settled down to wait, looking round to see if Alan and Tommy were there. They'd be at a different box, but still. Then he stared.

Up at the front of the queue was the tall dark girl he'd seen in the pub on Monday night. That seemed years ago. She was laughing and joking with someone in the next queue. Just at that moment she half turned and her eyes met Tucker's. In a split second he knew she'd recognised him. But the smile vanished from her face and she turned away instantly. Later the queue moved up and the girl walked past him. He knew she'd seen him, but her glance was turned away. So what?

At the counter he tried to exchange light conversation with the girl with the neat blouse and hair do, but he made no impression.

'Fill this form in, please.'

'But I filled that one in on Tuesday.'

'That was a BI form. This is a BIC. Take it round to Social Security.'

'What a waste of time.'

'If you want to get your benefit, then you need to fill it in.'

'Yeah, if I ever get any.'

'You won't if you don't fill the form in.'

Tucker took the form. As he turned, the next man in the queue grinned at him.

'You'll just have to cross her off your list, mate.'

Tucker walked outside. Paddy was still there.

'Hello, Peter, then. I see you've joined the toiling masses.'

'Wish I had, Paddy. Are you out of work, then?'

Paddy smiled: 'No, I'm not. I'm doing this for a friend. Just to give a hand, like.'

Tucker took a leaflet and walked away reading it.

'Fight for the Right to Work' said the leaflet.

They must be joking.

By the time Tucker had been back to the Social Security and queued up there, it was 12.30. The Careers Office was shut for lunch and he'd missed his appointment.

But his luck wasn't entirely out. When he returned to the Office in the afternoon, the Careers Officer greeted him like an old friend.

'Peter, isn't it? Peter Jenkins? Look, my name's Metcalfe, but call me Terry.'

Oh, if you insist, mate, thought Tucker, but it wasn't very encouraging.

Terry improved though, as the interview went on. When all the questions had been asked about A levels, O levels, CSEs, favourite subjects, hobbies, what you liked doing, what you didn't, he put the papers on one side and said.

23

'Do you want my honest opinion, Peter?'

What would his dishonest opinion be like?

'I'd go back to school, if I were you, for another year, to get some more qualifications.'

If you were me, mate, you wouldn't suggest anything so stupid.

'Look Peter, here are the figures for this area. Out of every hundred school leavers, thirty-five have got jobs, ten are on Youth Opportunities Programme work, thirteen are out of work, eight have gone to college, and thirty-three have gone back into the sixth form.'

'I don't want to go back to school.'

He must have spoken with some force, because Terry said, 'All right, all right, Peter. We'll do our best to find you something. What line shall we look at first?'

Tucker thought: 'Oh – building, painting, decorating, anything in that line.'

Terry began to run through the cards in the long box at the side of his desk. He was used to this and the card edges flicked under his fingers like an outboard motor. But he was shaking his head.

'Look Peter, come in first thing Monday morning. The earlier the better. You know, the old bird and worm business.'

Who was the worm?

Tucker suddenly had an idea: 'Look what about one of those YOP things. I know they're dead useless as jobs, but they're better than nothing.'

'Don't knock 'em, Peter. Some of them are not bad. But I'm afraid, it's no for the moment.'

'Why not.'

'You have to be out of work for six weeks first. Then we can fix you up.'

Tucker made a quick calculation. How long was it to October 15. He made it five weeks. That was no use, was it?

He said, "See you," to Terry and walked out. It was getting on for four o'clock. What next? Swimming, making parsnip wine, or watering the pot plants.

Not knowing quite what he was doing, he went round to the swimming pool. It was closed for repairs.

But in the club, he met a couple of old mates from school and won two quid at pool. That made £2.95.

Ah well. Maybe tomorrow his Bond would come up. Now £100,000 at 8¾ per cent, what was that?

Day Six

11.00 hours. The Famous Three were in the caff. Tommy held up a newspaper.

'This bloke here says they should lower the voting age to give a voice to the young unemployed.'

He read on: 'To avoid the social dangers that come from teenage despair and alienation.'

Tucker took the paper from him.

'You're putting us on, they never have stuff like that on Page 3.'

He studied the news item.

'Yeah, point is, who would you vote for, if you had the vote?'

Alan shook his head: 'Waste of time, mate, they're all the same.'

'Right on,' added Tommy. 'What they need is a few Molotov Cocktails up 'em.'

Tucker jeered: 'Bomber Watson? I don't see it. I can just imagine you in the pig van, saying, 'But Officer, honestly I needed those five dozen milk bottles, I'm on a diet.'

Alan finished his coffee. 'What are we going to do, anyway?'

'What d'you mean – vote or revolution?'

'Nah. What shall we do today?'

'No sweat,' said Tucker, pulling out his booklet. 'It's all here.'

The others stared as he began to read.

'Do the housework. Water the pot plants. Go swimming.'

He stopped. They looked at him pityingly. Then he said.

'Hey look, this we *can* do.'

'What?'

'In the library. Look in the job columns in the papers. Come on. You've got a better idea?'

Reluctantly, they came. The library reading room was empty save for two old chaps who looked as though they'd spent the night there.

'O.K.,' said Tucker, taking charge. 'You do the dailies, I'll do the evenings.'

'There isn't an evening today. That's yesterday's.'

'So, who's going job-snatching on Friday nights?'

For a while there was silence, broken only by the rustling of turning pages, then Tommy spoke: 'Hey, here we are: "Trainee technician."'

'Where's that?'

'Forget it, must have four 'O' levels.'

'Earn £10,000 in your first year of training.'

'Get off. Let's see. Look, 23-plus.'

'This is it. School leavers – a career in science. Jesus, five 'O' levels and A level chemistry and biology.'

'What about this? Under 35.'

'That's us.'

'Five feet four.'

'That's you. What's it for?'

'Hair modelling. But you've got to have size 10-12.'

'That let's you out.'

'Hey, what's C.O.M. trainee?'

'That's computer – let's see. Hey, 18 years of age. No, you missed the small print, 'A' level required.'

'What's this J.C.B. operator?'

'No problem, I've years of experience . . .'

'Only tax exempt and thirty per cent persons need apply.'

'Thirty per cent? I'm working my way down.'

'Ah,' burst out Alan, 'this is a load of garbage. You can get brain damage looking through all these.'

'Keep at it,' responded Tucker. 'Here's one for you.'

'Where? Topless waitress? Listen – Tucker!'

'You're better topless than any woman, Alan.'

Tucker grabbed Alan's shirt and pulled it out. Alan smacked Tucker's head. One of the old men put a furious face round the corner of the reading stands and the three, choking with suppressed laughter, went back to their reading.

'Despatch rider, any bike, beginners welcome, £200 plus a week. You could go for that, Tucker.'

'Does it say provisional licence, mate?'

'It does not, I fear.'

'Well, then, you may stuff it, sir.'

'Much obliged.'

Tommy suddenly crowed:

'Here it is. Toilet attendant, sober, fit, alert, courteous, smart appearance.'

'Hey, how many 'O' levels?'

'Get lost. You need an honours degree for that.'

'This is it,' called Alan, 'Wang Operator.'

'Wang Operator?' Tucker's voice rose in disbelief.

'That's what it says. Must be experienced.'

'Stand aside mate. Nobody's faster on the wang than me.'

'Show us your testimonial then.'

'What, right away? Won't a photo do?'

Amid the uproar, the inner door to the reading room opened. A young, soberly dressed man in heavy spectacles stood in the doorway.

'If there is any more of this noise, I'll have to ask you to leave. Other library users are complaining.'

He closed the door. Tucker jerked his head and the three headed for the street.

Alan turned to Tucker.

'See the advantage of qualifications, mate?'

'What advantage?'

'Have your 'O' and 'A' levels and you get to push the starving masses around.'

'You're not starving.'

'I am mate. Come on, let's go somewhere, where they do decent meals free.'

'Like where?'

'Like home.'

Day Seven

Tucker spent a quiet Sunday morning having a row with his Mum, then with his Dad.

The row with his Mum started when he had laid his various bike parts neatly out around his room, after rescuing them from the box where they had been dumped on the balcony. At the high point Tucker knew what was coming. She was going to say, 'It was bad enough when you were out at school, now when you're hanging about all . . .'

'Look Mum,' he said. 'if you could let me have five quid

from next week's money, I could get a set of points, and then I could get the bike going and most of this stuff would be gone from here anyway.'

'What next week's money?'

'We-ell, that ten you're letting me have every week till my giro comes.'

'Hasn't it come yet?'

'No, as a matter of fact it hasn't.'

His Dad who must have been listening from the kitchen where he was reading the Sunday papers suddenly joined in.

'Are you sure you have signed on?'

'Of course, I'm sure,' blazed Tucker. 'I've been up to the Labour three times, the Social Security twice, the Job Centre three times and the Careers Office twice. I'm sick of the sight of the bleeding places.'

'Watch your language.'

'It's all right for you to talk. You're in the lifeboat aren't you.'

Tucker's Dad suddenly appeared in the doorway. He looked about to throw a fit. Then suddenly he changed his mind.

'You can't buy yourself a set of points anyway. They're shut.'

'All right.'

Tucker's dad reached into his pocket and handed over a five pound note. As Tucker took it, his father suddenly produced another one and passed it over.

'Sorry Dad. I can't help the job situation can I?'

'Didn't say you could. But you've got an alternative, haven't you? Look, why don't you pack this social lark in, and go back to school?'

Tucker shook his head:

'You said I could have till October 15th.'

His Dad shrugged and went back to his paper.

That afternoon Tucker took his bike out on the backs. There was a clear 70-80 yard run behind the garages. After three hours work, and some stealthy trips up and down to his room for bits and pieces, the bike fired. Its roar rumbled round the flats and windows opened here and there. The engine cut out. The windows closed again. Tucker tried again.

It happened two or three times more. But finally, when the light had nearly gone, the bike started – and kept going. Tucker took it down the backs again. Then as the windows started to open once more, he swung it out and on to the road outside the flats.

Three hundred yards down the road he stopped, quicker than he had started. It was handling like a ruptured stoat. He wheeled it back slowly, thinking hard. By the time he was back at the flats again, he had worked out what his trouble was. The oil seals on the right hand rear shocker had gone. That was ten quid up his jumper, at the very least.

Ho hum.

Day Eight

Tucker was down at the Job Centre early that day. But so were a lot of others. He'd never seen the place so busy. And not just school leavers; older blokes and women, one with a push chair, some looking eager, some looking anxious, some looking, well, sick. He recognised some people from the flats. One bloke nodded to him, but didn't seem to want to talk. Tucker couldn't blame him. Who wanted to be seen in this club?

As he left he bumped into Alan, on his way to the Career Centre.

'They told me to come down early on Monday,' he said. 'Coming?'

'Why not? Where's Watson?'

'Dunno. Said something about meeting somebody. Were you with him when he met that bit in the pub, Tucker?'

'Yeah, but I thought she – he's a silly sod, is Tommy. Likes to live dangerously doesn't he?'

'Well that's *his* trouble.'

'As long as we don't get involved.'

'Too right.'

At the Careers Centre Terry greeted them with a grin.

'Glad you could come in, Peter, Alan.'

He'd remembered the names, good lad. The only problem was, he called Tucker, Alan and Alan, Peter. Still they had several years to sort that out.

'Nothing in the painting, decorating line, Peter, but something close by.'

'Oh. What's that?'

'Don't sound so suspicious. It's an estate agent's. They want two juniors, learn the business, day release to study.'

'Why us?' asked Alan.

'First come, first served on this one. Look, he wants to see applicants at two this afternoon.'

His eyes flickered over Tucker's front.

'Don't worry, Terry. We'll dress ourselves up nicely, won't we, Alan?'

Terry grinned. 'Sorry, but it could make all the difference.'

At two that afternoon Tucker and Alan, half strangled in tie and collar with all the trimmings walked into the estate agent's. The girl at the desk rolled her eyes when she saw them.

'In there,' she said. 'If you can find room.'

'But they said at the Careers Office there were only us two,' protested Alan.

'Ah yes, but he's been advertising as well. And he's been on to Job Centres in other areas as well. He doesn't take chances, Mr Purser doesn't.'

'Can't wait to meet him." muttered Tucker.

But they had to. In the other room there were a dozen other people, young men and women, all most unsuitably dressed for a Monday afternoon. As Tucker and Alan walked in there was an exchange of glances, a chuckle or two, then an embarrassed silence reigned once more.

A red light flashed over an inner door. It opened and a young man walked out. He raised his eyebrows at the others in the room as he walked across and disappeared through the outer door. The red light flashed again and a hearty voice from the next room called: 'Next one, if you don't mind.'

And so, at ten minute intervals, it went on through the afternoon. Twice Alan was for leaving, but Tucker held him back.

'We're wasting our time – all these others in front.'

'Listen mate, when he sees us – well, when he sees me, he's going to forget 'em all.'

At 4.15 Alan and Tucker were left alone in the room. The red light flashed again. Alan looked at Tucker.

'After you, mate,' said Tucker.

Alan went in, and a little later, came out again. His face was expressionless. He merely jerked his head to the inner door, as the light flashed once more. Tucker went in.

Behind the large mahogany desk at the centre of the inner room, sat a man in check suit, balding, red faced. As Tucker sat down, a wave of gin and tonic reached him from the other side of the desk.

'You're Jenkins, are you? Got your bumf from the

32

Careers Office. Well let's see now, this is a job that really calls for considerable qualifications.'

'The careers officer said . . .' Tucker began, but Purser ploughed on. 'But as I often say to my fellow members of the Rotary Club, our problem is that we have these young people and we have to do something about them. There aren't many people, I can assure you, who would give up their whole afternoon to interviewing young applicants, but I happen to be one of them.

'How some people like to set all kinds of tests for applicants, all kinds of psychological how's your father. But not me.'

He paused and taking a cigar from the desk in front of him, lit it with the large lighter that stood on the desk pad. The cigar had been lit many times that afternoon and the smell wafted across to Tucker's nose to join the gin and tonic.

'Not me. I pride myself that I can spot the person I need right away. No good trying to fool me by dressing up and all that, it's the chap underneath I'm interested in.'

Tucker's mind boggled. His eyes glazed over, as Purser went on.

'One of our problems is, to be frank, and I don't mind being frank with you, man to man – I know I'm old enough to be your father but . . .'

The voice bumbled on. Tucker jerked. He was almost falling asleep. He heard Purser say: 'One question none of these trendies can answer is why don't the schools prepare the pupils for the life they'll have to face, why don't they prepare them for the jobs they're going to fill.'

'What jobs?' Tucker heard his own voice cut across Purser's.

'What's that?'

'I said, what jobs. I mean I don't see them. You want two juniors. Fifteen people came. What happens to the unlucky thirteen? What should they have done at school, anyway, give us lessons in drawing the dole?'

He got to his feet. Purser stared at him.

'And don't say—'I'll let you know' because I know you won't. You've been getting your kicks bending our ears all afternoon.'

He walked out, closing the door. As he reached the outer room Alan looked at his face and burst out laughing.

'Stupid great tit,' fumed Tucker.

'Come on mate, calm down. It won't do any good.' said Alan. 'I'll buy you a coffee.'

As they sat in the cafe across the road from the estate agent's, they heard a voice behind them.

'I don't know about these young people on the dole. They seem to be able to dress well enough, don't they.'

Alan got up, his face furious. Tucker grabbed him and pulled him down again.

'Calm down mate. It won't do any good. Drink your coffee.'

Day Nine AM

Tucker met Alan that morning on his way to the Careers Office.

'What's the rush?'

'I'm just going in to tell Terry Bleeding Metcalfe what he can do with interviews like that Purser one in future,' answered Alan.

'I'll join you.'

But someone had got in first.

As they walked into the Careers Office reception, Jill, the secretary, her face pale, was dialling away furiously at the phone. From inside Terry's room came the sound of shouting and the sudden snap of a breaking chair.

Tucker looked at Alan. Without a word they barged in. Someone standing with their back to the door was thrown aside. They saw Terry at the side of his desk and in front of him, arm raised, a bloke in black jacket and jeans, a young bloke, but big and nasty with it. A second bloke was standing a yard or two away holding his hand to his head. Alan's shoulder on the door must have given him a slight headache. On the floor in front of them lay a chair with the leg snapped off.

The two turned and stared at Alan and Tucker, then at Terry, as if weighing up the odds. Then from the outer office came Jill's voice over the phone: 'Is that the police?'

At the magic word, the two exchanged a quick glance, then throwing themselves past Tucker and Alan, they barged out of the room. A second later the outer door slammed and running feet crunched on the concrete walk outside.

Terry let out his breath and came to the front of the desk to pick up the broken chair.

'What was all that about?' asked Tucker.

Terry sat down and waved Tucker and Alan to the two undamaged chairs near the desk.

'What do you think? No jobs. At least no jobs they can hold. The SS people are pressurising them, so they're pressurising me. But I can't see them getting anything. To be honest, I'll be glad when they change the rules and let people like them draw their money without pushing them to chase after non-existent work.'

'Hey, this job's dangerous,' said Alan. 'Are you going to be all right? I mean what happens when you go home tonight, say?'

Terry grinned. 'Oh, I can look after myself on the street. It's just that brawling with clients in the office is bad for promotion prospects.'

He re-arranged the scattered papers on his desk.

'Now . . .' he began.

Suddenly the door to the outer office opened. Jill stood in the doorway. Immediately behind her were two men in uniform, one a sergeant. They stepped past her.

'Are these the two, Mr . . .?' demanded the sergeant glancing sharply at Tucker and Alan.

Terry got up again: 'No sergeant. Certainly not. They arrived just in time. The others have gone.'

'I see. Do you know who they were? Names, anything?' The sergeant looked again at Tucker, as if giving him the photofit treatment.

Terry shook his head: 'They were only here for a moment, sergeant. They just came in off the street and started causing a row. It's quite all right, I assure you. I'm sorry that we troubled you.'

Reluctantly, the police withdrew, tramping through the outer office. When they heard the police car start up outside, Tucker and Alan turned to Terry again.

'You knew who they were,' said Alan.

Terry shrugged. 'That's not my branch. I'm sure they're well known. But I have to deal with all kinds of stroppy individuals - including people who slag out prospective employers.'

He looked at Tucker, who grinned, embarrassed.

'Mr Purser was on the phone this morning. I have had a busy day so far, I can tell you. He was very put out.'

'Then he can join the club,' said Tucker. 'Has he given anybody the job.'

'No, it seems nobody suited him.'

'Load of hot air, I reckon.'

'Look, Peter. I'm just supposed to help people find work and careers, but now and then I do give other sorts of advice. Can I ask you to remember one thing – 'Keep Calm'. It may be a long haul, getting work. You're going to

36

meet a lot of people who have power. You can't sort them all out.'

He lifted a file from his desk: 'There's something here, if you care to have a look at it.'

'What's that? Five A levels and a degree for window cleaning?' Terry shook his head: 'No previous experience, no qualifications. Benmore Agricultural. Six vacancies for Trainee in Lifestock Management. £55 a week.'

'Where's it – Wales or Scotland?'

'Well, it's a bit out. Train ride. But they make a travel allowance,' he paused, 'payable at the end of the first fortnight.'

Tucker and Alan looked at each other. Shrugged.

'Shall we give it a run?' asked Tucker. 'We could take Watson with us. The fresh air'll do him good.'

Alan looked doubtful.

Tucker made a quick cast up in his mind. £55 a week. If he did a fortnight he could have enough to satisfy his Dad, fix his bike, then look around at his ease for another fortnight. He mentally rubbed his hands. He stood up and held out his hand.

'I'll have a go,' he said.

Slowly Alan got up.

'O.K.'.

As they left the Careers Office he turned to Tucker.

'This had better be very good.'

'Good, you're joking. It's just better than watering the pot plants and brewing parsnip wine, that's all.'

Alan stopped on the pavement and turned to Tucker.

'Listen, mate, never mind that for a minute. I don't want to bother you. But Terry isn't the only one who knows that herbert who was in the office this morning.'

'What's that supposed to mean?'

'You know him, Tucker.'

'No I don't. I hardly saw his face, he went out so fast.'

'I did, though. It was your old friend Benson – Booga Benson. So, watch your back, Jenkins, and your front as well.'

Tucker shrugged: 'So? The place is big enough. Anyway, come on let's get Watson and head for the sticks.'

'What, today?'

'Why not. Get half a day in – that'll be £5.50 less deductions.'

'You're mad.'

'You coming, or not?'

'OK, but like I said, it has to be good.'

Day Nine PM

A light drizzle was falling when the Famous Three got off the train and headed for Benmore Agricultural. The ticket collector told them, with a grin: 'Just down the road.'

It was, three miles. But they were in luck. A huge container wagon drew up alongside them on the wet tarmac. The driver leaned down from the cab.

'Where you going, son?'

'Benmore Agricultural.'

The driver grinned.

'Oh, there. I've given plenty of lifts to there.'

(What was the joke about this place?)

They crowded into the cab. The driver looked them over as he started the engine.

'Trainees?' he asked. They nodded.

'Ah well, better than the dole. Been out of work long?'

'Since we left school.' said Tucker. It sounded more impressive.

'Bad bloody business, mate. Just like when I was a kid

before the war. Thousands hanging about, nothing to do, nowhere to go. Mind you, they pay you a bit more, don't they?'

'Haven't noticed.' said Alan.

'All depends what you're used to,' said the driver, swinging the huge truck round the farm tractor and trailer trundling along the narrowing road.

'Where I was born, they had a riot, the unemployed. Police horses, truncheons, broken windows, the lot. And you know what it was about – they cut the dole by threepence a week. Three bloody pence a week.'

He slowed down and pulled in.'Here y'are.'

'I can't see any farm?' said Tommy.

'Down the track,' answered the driver.

They looked out over a bare stretch of countryside, flat and hedgeless with big grey oblong blocks.

'Looks more like a prison camp,' said Tucker.

'All according to taste,' said the driver. 'Good luck, lads.'

Ten minutes later they were greeted in front of the farm office by an immensely tall, thin, grey-faced man in a white coat.

'You from Careers? Just hang on a bit. I'll get your gear.'

They looked around the concrete waste. On either side rose huge concrete and metal walls. All was quiet, save for the steady beat of machinery somewhere close by.

'Weird, isn't it? No hens, no cows, no milkmaids.'

'Well, there must be lifestock. Else what do we manage?'

The thin man returned, carrying a huge pile of yellow plastic clothing and green wellies.

'Get these on.'

'Do we have to?' said Tommy eyeing the clothing with distaste. 'Doesn't match my hair.'

'You're going to be glad of it.' Next he handed them white face masks.

Then he jerked his thumb. 'Come on.'

He led them behind the first building and pointed to a large truck on rubber wheels. From it projected the handles of brushes and broad bladed shovels.

He pulled open the huge door to the great shed. A wave of powerful stench, a mixture of ammonia and worse things hit them. A small motorised truck carrying two young lads in white coats swept out past them.

'Hey, why do they have white coats and we have this yellow gear?'

'They're on feeding stuffs. They have to keep very clean.'

Light was dawning. Tucker said, 'And what are we on?'

The dark face of the thin man suddenly shone with an awful smile.

'You're going to start on the arse end and work your way up.' he said. 'Come on.'

Day Nine PPM

Tucker got home after dark, but the family knew he was coming. His mother made him stand on the balcony while she got him a change of clothes.

He fell into bed like a dead man. The alarm clock was broken but his father generously promised to wake him at 06.15 the next day.

Day Ten

Tommy didn't turn up. Tucker and Alan shovelled pig shit for eight hours with a break for lunch—cheese sandwiches and tea all smelling of high protein.

Tucker got home after dark. Now the neighbours knew he was coming.

Day Eleven

Alan didn't turn up. Tucker shovelled pig shit until lunch time.

Then he went to the office and after an argument, got paid off—£13-50 after deductions.

After that he went home, had a bath and crawled into bed, just remembering in time to leave his Dad a note cancelling the alarm call.

He slept until mid-morning on Day Twelve.

Day Twelve

Began badly, but got better as it went on.

When Tucker arrived at the Employment Office (late) his friend at Box Six looked at her list and said: 'Oh, what are you doing here?'

'I'm signing on, aren't I?'

'You shouldn't be. You're working. We've had your Parts 1 and 2 back from you.'

'Well, I'm not working, am I? I couldn't keep away from you.'

'You'll have to see the supervisor.'

'I'd rather see you.'

'But he wants to see you. Next please.'

Tucker had a tense five minutes in the supervisor's office. Tense because he was trying to remember Terry's advice, 'Keep calm.' It seemed he was a bad lad for walking off the job without giving himself a chance to get used to it.

Get used to it? What happened to you, when you got used to that?

But because this was the first offence, he would just lose three day's benefit. He'd be allowed a new attendance card without doing the yo-yo routine between Employment Office and Social Security again. But he'd have to sign on again next Friday, instead of Friday fortnight.

Simmering, Tucker marched out. In the queue he passed the tall dark girl, but did not even look at her. Outside on the pavement, he spotted old Paddy handing out leaflets.

'Hello Peter, then. How are you?'

'Since you ask, Paddy, I'm not. Give us some of those will you?'

Tucker stood with Paddy for twenty mintues, helping hand out leaflets. He didn't know what exactly was in them, but didn't care.

'Do you take time off every week just to hand these things out, Paddy?'

'I've all the time in the world just now Peter. They gave me my marching orders last week.'

'What for, Paddy?'

'Taking time off to hand these things out.' Paddy grinned.

Tucker shook his head. Paddy wanted his bumps feeling.

Looking after everybody else's job except his own.

'Peter, can you just hold these while I go inside?'

'Bit late for signing on, Paddy.'

'No, it's the only place around where you can have a civilised slash. I'll be back in a few minutes.'

It seemed Paddy had barely vanished inside the building when Tucker heard the grind of brakes at his back. He turned. A police car had pulled up a yard away from him. And leaning out of the near-side window was a police sergeant.

'You, lad. What have you got there? Come here. Quick. Move.'

Keep calm.

Tucker stepped up to the window and showed the leaflets. The sergeant took them from him. Their eyes met.

'I've seen you before somewhere, haven't I?'

Tucker said nothing.

'Yes I think we have. The little bundle at the Careers place on Tuesday. You're very mobile, aren't you?'

The sergeant jerked his head.

'In the back.'

Tucker was about to abandon his Keep Calm policy when someone spoke behind him.

'Excuse me, officer. Just a moment.'

Tucker turned. The sergeant looked up.

On the pavement stood a middle-aged man, neat in charcoal-grey suit, with reddish face, neat military-type moustache and snow-white hair carefully waved. In his hand he held a maroon leather despatch case.

'Don't wish to interfere, but in the interests of justice, officer. This young man may have been the victim of a confidence trick.'

The sergeant examined the new arrival closely. The man suddenly produced a card from his inside pocket and held it out.

'Charles Barraclough, Flag Enterprises. I just happened to be passing. I saw an older man ask this young chap here to hold the bundle of leaflets. I'm sure he only did it to oblige. Great pity if being polite in this day and age lands you in trouble, wouldn't you say?'

'Are you sure, sir?'

'Absolutely sergeant. My guess is the other chap saw you people coming. They're very fly, you know. I've met them in the services, you know. Have to be up very early to catch 'em.'

Hey, was that true? wondered Tucker. Had Paddy lumbered him? The old sod. He looked round. There was no sign of Paddy.

'Very well,' the sergeant looked frustrated. He gave Tucker a stare. 'We'll leave it for now. But – just watch it.'

The police car drew away. Tucker drew a deep breath and turned to thank his saviour.

Barraclough smiled showing a double line of teeth as white as his hair.

'Saved in the nick of time, eh? Perhaps nick isn't the right word ... how about a cup of coffee, – er ...?'

'Peter. Peter Jenkins.'

'Splendid, Peter. Across the way.'

As they sat down with their coffee, Barraclough leaned over to Tucker.

'May I offer you some advice? Steer clear of chaps like that.'

'What, the police sergeant?'

'Ha ha, very good, Peter. Glad to see you have a sense of humour. No I mean people who promise instant solutions to unemployment – revolution and all that. Won't work. Do you know what the real solution to unemployment is, Peter?'

Tucker shook his head. No he didn't.

'Enterprise, Peter, enterprise.' Barraclough showed his

card again. 'This means what is says. Take steps. Do something. Earn money. Don't waste time.'

'How?' Tucker suddenly felt he was in for a long spiel from another old fart like Purser.

Barraclough laughed. 'Don't think I'm going to lecture you, Peter. I'm going to put a proposition to you. You see it was pure coincidence the police happened to be there. I was just about to speak to you anyway.'

'Oh, why?'

'Don't be so suspicious. No, correction, be suspicious. Don't just take anyone's word. Let 'em show the colour of their money, I say. Now I thought, a young man with the guts and initiative to hand out inflammatory leaflets, must have the qualities I need in Barraclough Enterprises.'

'What do they do?'

'In a word. We sell. We sell door to door. Don't turn your nose up. There is money door to door, because behind those doors are ladies with housekeeping money to spend. You bring them what they need, they pay. The particular line I want to interest you in is soft drinks. Do you know how many gallons of orange, lemon, cola and so on the average family gets through a year?'

'Is this commission work?' asked Tucker.

'Right on, it is commission work. 60p commission on an order of three bottles. You would have to be very slow to clear less than £40 even in the first week. Especially when the housewives know you are a school leaver. They have a soft spot – especially for a good-looking chap like you.'

He paused, thinking something over: 'Another idea occurs to me. Do you have any mates?'

'A couple.'

'How would you like to set up a team to run one of our sub-depots. They are operated from houses and flats, and the agent in charge of a depot gets a special percentage 15p on every order, making 75p. We supply the goods. You

45

organise the sales. Look, take a note of this address – 15, Harcourt, Bracewell Road. Get hold of your friends, and,' Barraclough looked at his watch, 'meet me there at 3pm. Now don't be late. On the dot. I don't have much time – I've a dozen other sub-depots to attend to.'

Barraclough got to his feet, held out his hand and shook Tucker's firmly. 'Don't be late,' he said and turning, marched briskly from the cafe.

It took Tucker an hour or so to locate Alan and Tommy and another hour to persuade them. But in the end, they agreed and at 3pm on the dot (why was Barraclough such a maniac for punctuality?) they reached the address. It was a block of flats, post-war but somewhat the worse for wear. At No 15, Barraclough opened the door and let them into a room which was bare except for lino and a square of carpet. He wasted no time.

'Surprised, eh? Well of course it's a flat, one of a number we rent, and then sub-let to our agents.'

'Sub-let?' said Tucker. He knew there'd be a catch.

'Of course, Peter, nothing's for nothing in this game. £5 a week rent for a sub-depot, but remember, agent's extra commission on thirty orders and your rent's paid.'

His voice lowered: 'Then there is another advantage. You and your mates can live here – as long as we have room to store the stock while you are getting it out to the customers.'

'What's the good of that?' asked Alan.

'What is the good, young man? How much are you people getting from the social security?'

'£16.85 a week.' said Tucker.

'That is because you are in the parental home. Once you have your own address, the amount will double. That will stand you in good stead until your earnings from sales begin to mount up. And most certainly they will.'

'O.K.,' said Tommy, 'I can see that. We don't have to actually sleep here anyway. But I know some kids who were nicked selling door to door.'

'Ha,' said Barraclough. 'That is the problem with amateurs. Hawkers' licenses.'

'Who pays for those,' demanded Tucker.

'You, I'm afraid, old boy. There are bound to be initial outlays.'

'How much?'

'Just under £5 each. But it's a passport to earning and independence. You'll be your own bosses remember. No other expenses.'

The lads looked at one another.

'Think it over,' said Barraclough and walked into the next room.

'That's twenty altogether,' said Alan. 'I've only got five.'

'I've only got four,' said Tommy.

Tucker looked at them: 'O.K., I'll put in the other eleven. But you owe me. Don't forget.'

Barraclough came back into the room. He looked at them.

'Still doubtful? That's not the way to start out in business. You have to take risks.'

'Ah, risks, O.K.,' said Alan, 'but what security have we got?'

Barraclough grinned: 'Good man.' He held out his hand. In it was a yale key and a green book.

'Here is the key to the sub-depot and your rent-book from Flag Enterprises. I've written in your names, or rather Peter's since we can't have more than one sub-agent per depot. But you can sort that out.'

He shook hands with them all.

'I'll be round, or one of my deputies, on Monday, with licences and your first supplies. Be ready at 9 a.m. sharp.'

'Can we move gear in here before then?' asked Tommy, his mind working, Tucker could see, on other possibilities.

'As soon as you like. No. Give me two hours to move one or two things out which you won't need. From this evening on.'

.He shook hands with them once more.

'I wish I were in your shoes now. To be starting out again. Good luck, lads. Remember, enterprise is the thing.'

As the door closed behind them, Tucker, Alan and Tommy stood on the landing.

'I hope we know what we're doing?' said Alan.

'Miserable sod,' said Tucker. 'Let's go and celebrate our career in business.'

'With what?' asked Tommy.

'I've got a couple of quid left. Come on.'

Day Thirteen

Lived up to its name – or number.

Tucker woke from a dream in which he had risen rapidly from star salesman to chairman of the Board of Flag Enterprises and was on his way to Buck House for the old shoulder tap, to hear banging on his bedroom door. It was mid-morning, the sun was shining through the window and his mother was calling.

'Peter, get up, Tommy wants you.'

Tucker heaved himself out of bed, pulled on pants and shirt and shuffled out into the kitchen. Tommy was there, but not sitting down. When he saw Tucker, he jerked his head and walked out on to the balcony. Baffled Tucker followed him.

No sooner was the door shut safely when Tommy turned on him with murder in his voice.

'You striped me up last night.'

'I did what? I did you a big favour, mate, I laid on an apartment for you. I let you use our sub-depot for evil purposes, that's what I did, but...'

'That key...'

'Yeah, the key...?'

'It didn't fit the door, did it? I suppose you had a big giggle in bed afterwards.'

Tucker laughed out loud, then stopped when he saw Tommy's expression.

'Sorry, old son. But the picture of you holding your bird on one arm, your mattress on the other and trying to open the door with your teeth was mildly amusing.'

'Listen, Tucker. That key does not fit the door.'

Tucker stopped laughing.

'So what did you do with the right one, mate?' Tommy fumed.

'Knock it off, Tommy. There was only one key. Barra-clough gave me a key with the rent book. That was the key I lent you. Listen, if you've bust it.'

Tommy held up his hand and thrust a key under Tucker's nose.

'That's it. Think yourself lucky I didn't come round last night and wake you up.'

'Think yourself lucky you didn't, son,' answered Tucker. Then he stopped. 'Listen, Tommy. Hang on while I phone Alan. We'll go down there.'

Ten minutes later Alan arrived and a quarter of an hour after that they were climbing the stairs to number 15 Faircourt. They were not alone as they came out on to the balcony. The small space was crowded with about a dozen blokes, all around their own age, waving arms and arguing.

Tucker shouldered his way through to the door.

49

'Do you mind, thank you.'

He pushed the key into the lock. It jammed half way in. The group behind him suddenly began to laugh. He swung round and glared. The bloke nearest stopped laughing.

'You know,' he said, 'it's actually funny watching somebody else do it.'

'What d'you mean, somebody else.'

The lad stuck his hand into his jeans pocket and waved a yale key in Tucker's face. Then from his jacket he pulled out a small green book.

'We've been set up. The lot of us.'

'S'right,' said another, 'he must have cleared two hundred quid.'

'Yeah, those rent books cost 35p each in Woolies. And the keys – he could have got those anywhere.'

'But Barraclough had the key to the flat himself.'

'Barra – who? His name was Sherratt.'

'No it wasn't,' interrupted another, 'it was "Montgomery".'

Are you sure it wasn't Prince Philip?'

'Could have been. He used every bleeding name in the phone book.'

'Anyway, no use hanging about. He's probably off somewhere else looking for a fresh supply of mugs.'

'I reckon we ought to keep our eye on this place. He'll probably come back later on. He can't keep any amount of places going can he?'

Footsteps sounded on the stairs below. Two men in boiler suits came on to the balcony. One carried a tool bag.

'Excuse us, if you don't mind,' he said as he eased his way to the door.

'What are you doing?' demanded one of the crowd.

'Changing the lock, that's what. Somebody nicked the key. The agent rang up last night – urgent job. So, if you don't mind.'

'That's it then. Twenty bloody quid up the wall.'

The crowd began to break up and drift down the stairs to the street.

Tucker looked sideways at Alan. 'What you looking so narky for? You weren't planning to spend the night there with someone?'

Alan looked at him dangerousy. 'I was going to take Susi out for a meal tonight.'

'Well, you can let her pay for once – don't be sexist.'

'Funny man.'

They strolled along the pavement to the High Road. Alan stopped and said: 'I've learnt one lesson from this carve up, Tucker!'

'Tell me.'

'Have nothing to do with any more of your stupid ideas.'

'Thank you – what are friends for, if you can't learn something from them?'

Day Fourteen

Tucker spent the morning looking at his bike. His bike looked back at him. It wouldn't even move, even with rear wheel wobble. He needed ten quid to fit it up. He had exactly £1.95 left. Twenty six days to go and he was worse off than when he'd started.

He'd nearly destroyed his back on that pig farm, old Paddy had sold him out to the Old Bill, Barraclough had ripped him off.

The Premium Bonds computer had let him down. He'd have been prepared to settle for a £25 prize at this stage.

Even the DHSS, the father and mother of all school leavers had deserted him. Not a sign of his giro cheque.

51

And when it did come, they'd have knocked off three days.

He went in doors. The light was going.

There wasn't even kids' television to watch.

If he had some pot plants, now . . .

Day Fifteen

On Day Fifteen it came. Not the £100,000 Premium Bond prize, not the £50,000, not even the £25. It was the magical green-and-white giro cheque, a total of £33.30 to see him, and his Mum, through the next fortnight.

Tucker went round to the post office. There was a queue. Everybody else had come to get their money, mothers with small kids running round and pulling bits and pieces from the displays, old ladies and gents with their pension books and one or two giro pushers like himself. It was all very matey. They all seemed to know each other. He could see himself growing old and grey lining up here every fortnight: 'How are you love? Not bad, can't complain. I was up last night though. Must have been something I ate. You have to be so careful.'

When he got away with his money, he had to do something quickly to cheer himself up. He went round smartly to the bike shop and parted with £10.45. Then he went home and sorted his money out. He put his mother's share on the working top in the kitchen, then spread his own share out. He had about £11.95 to last him the fortnight. Something had to turn up. He made himself a cup of tea.

He found himself thinking about the day's routine. That stupid leaflet from the Careers Office wasn't so stupid. But he scrubbed out the idea of job hunting, along with swimming and watering the pot plants. Today he was going to spend on the bike.

For a couple of hours he worked on the dodgey shock absorber until he was sure it was right. Then he wheeled the bike on to the backs. Once more the thrilling, pulsing roar of the engine shattered the peace of the flats, as he took the machine up and down the eighty yard dirt stretch behind the garages.

Someone must have been reading his thoughts. As he made his fifth run a window went up in one of the flats and somebody shouted out: 'Why don't you bring the bloody machine up on our balcony so we can hear it properly?'

Sarcasm was wasted on T. Jenkins. He called back cheerfully.

'No thanks! I can't get a good enough run up there.'

There was a silence, then the head and shoulders of a man still in his pyjamas appeared in the window opening.

'Listen, would you like me to come round and wrap that bike round your neck? I'm on shift work, when am I supposed to sleep? Why don't you go and get yourself some useful work?'

That was too many questions to answer. Apart from which he looked nasty enough, and big enough to follow up his offer.

Tucker waved to him and took the bike out on to the road.

He didn't wave back.

Over to the caff. No sign of Alan or Tommy. Tucker allowed himself a leisurely egg on toast with beans, then drove round to Alan's place.

He found Alan busy helping his Dad load the van. He didn't offer to join in. He had a feeling Alan would be at it for the day and what's more a feeling that it would be under the Old Pal's Act or for very little reward. That was the trouble with having a Dad who ran a business; they tended to rip the family off.

He cruised around the streets looking idly to left and

right. Then suddenly, in mid-afternoon he saw something which made him pull in to the side of the road. A gap in a tall corrugated iron fence showed an open space, below road level. What was more it was concreted over. A lot of rubble had been pushed up to the sides leaving a wide circle of hard ground.

At the far end a long ramp, also concreted, led up to a gate in the fence. He swung the bike and rode round the side street. But the gate was padlocked. Back he went to the other side. The gap was narrow, but with a bit of manipulative skill and brute force he got the machine through and, with a yell, sent the bike surging down the dirt slope on to the concrete apron below.

As he circled, running up and down the gears (the bike was running very nicely now) he noticed the shed. It was in the far corner – about as big as a couple of the garages back home. He approached it to find that this too was padlocked. He pulled the bike over and looked through the window.

Inside was a large car, the body work taped over. There was a smell of paint in the air. Someone was using this as a re-spray shop. There was no notice outside. He wondered idly who it might be, then shrugged. Nothing to lose sleep over.

For the rest of the afternoon he ran the bike round, then took it home and put it away.

On the box they were showing the kids' serial about the school.

He settled down to watch. Happy Days.

Day Sixteen

To the Job Centre nice and early. Quite a few people there. Some Tucker recognised. They greeted him like old friends. Even the bloke at the desk looked up, nodded and, without a word, handed him a blank sheet of paper.

There were some other old friends there, too. The 'brass gravity die caster, £100 p.w.' the 'wood machinist, fully skilled', the 'junior sales rep. £7,500, selling background', the 'second chef, city and guilds', the five years' experience stove enamel sprayer, the middle aged bricklayer. But the healthy cashier and the dish washer had gone.

So had Tucker's interest by now. He placed the blank sheet of paper, still blank, back in front of the bloke at the desk, and walked out.

Back home, he put on the kettle and called a meeting of his finance and general purposes committee. He had roughly 80p a day for the next fortnight. What was that? – a fishburger and a litre of petrol, a pint and a small packet of peanuts, not quite a seat at the flicks. The array of options dazzled him. He called the meeting to a close and went out to the backs with his bike.

Just as he was starting up, he remembered the Incredible Shift Worker and shoved the bike round to the road. He headed for the place he'd discovered yesterday. Approaching by the side streets he was surprised to find the gate unpadlocked.

With a yell he set the bike down the ramp. For a split second he felt the wind tear at his jacket. Then he saw something which made him brake and skid to a stop a few yards away from the workshop hut.

In front of it stood a battered grey open truck. The

registration was M – that must be the last alphabet but one.

He looked again. To the side of the hut four lads in overalls and masks were working on the spray job he had seen through the shed window. At the sound of his skid they looked up and stopped work. One, tall and lanky, came towards him. The goggles and mask concealed his face, but Tucker could see he was black.

'What do you want?' The tone wasn't friendly.

Tucker pondered a moment. He had the feeling he was about to be seen off. He doubted their right to do it. But he was in less doubt about their being able to do it. On the other hand, there was room around here for everybody. Softly, softly might be the touch.

He raised the vizor on his helmet.

At the same time the black lad pushed up his goggles. Both stared.

'Hey, Tucker.'

It was Hughes, from school, one of Doylie's victims that Alan, Tucker and Benny had bailed out in the old days.

They grinned at each other.

'What 're you doing, guy?'

Tucker made a face.

'Not much. I was just going to run the bike around here a bit.'

'Why not?' Then Hughes hesitated. 'Hang about though. Better wait and see what Roller says.'

One of the other lads in the gang called. Hughes half turned and waved, then turned back.

'Who's Roller?' asked Tucker.

'Oh, Roller. He runs the operation. We've got a group. They let us use this place . . . there are three.' He stopped, remembering something: 'You see Benny lately, Tucker?'

No, Tucker hadn't seen Benny Green since school.

'I thought he'd gone pro. You know, the Reserves.'

Hughes shook his head.

'Later, maybe. Now he's back in school, doing O's, man. His pa made him, you know.'

Tucker stared, in silence. How many more of the old lot were back there?

Another shout came from the spraying group: 'Roller!'

Hughes suddenly left Tucker and went back to the car body. Tucker looked up the slope he'd just skidded down, as a whirring, crunching sound grew louder in his ears.

Over the crest of the slope, like a surf rider, came a bloke on skates. Hughes was tall. This bloke was taller, and broader, though not older. He wore a black beret and shirt, and his jeans were tucked into knee length stockings. From the side of his head hung the leads of a Walkman. He came down fast, faster than Tucker on his bike and headed right towards him. Tucker braced both feet on the ground as Roller came closer and then braked, swivelling in a shower of sparks to a stop a foot away. He was head and shoulders above Tucker. He did not look welcoming.

'You want, something, friend?'

Hughes came towards them again pushing up his goggles.

'This is Tucker, from school. I told you, Roller, with Benny. He's all right. I know him.'

'I don't.' Roller looked at Tucker again waiting for his answer. Tucker suddenly felt irritated.

'I came down to run my bike round. There's room. You people aren't using the lot, are you?'

Roller nodded to Hughes who went back to his work.

'We're busy, see. Got this job to finish by five o'clock tonight.'

'We don't want anybody jacking around here with bikes.'

Tucker had an idea suddenly.

'Do you do many of these jobs – re-sprays and that?'

Roller weighed his answer: 'Now and then. When we get them.'

'Do you do bikes?'

A trace of a smile came on to Roller's face: 'Why, you want your's fixing?'

'Nah,' said Tucker. 'I can look after that myself. I was just thinking about doing other bikes. Is there much in it?'

Roller's smile vanished.

'Please yourself whose bike you fix, friend, but just don't do it round here, O.K? Round here we make our bread.'

He swung away and over to the others without a word.

Tucker paused a moment, then started his bike and drove up the ramp. The black lads, busy at the car body did not even look up as he went.

As he rode home, though, Tucker was thinking.

That idea was worth working on.

Day Seventeen

'Alan? That you Alan?'

'Yeah, Tucker.'

'Listen, there was this bloke, went for a ride on his bike.'

'He didn't. Tucker! How extraordinary.'

'And he took his mate on the pillion, see.'

'He never.'

'You're going to be sorry if I decide not to tell you the rest.'

'Try me.'

'Anyway, they went out on the motorway. It was freezing cold and his mate didn't have proper gear on. So they stopped at a service station and his mate took his coat off and put it on back to front, and the other bloke fastened it up round his back. Keep the wind out, see.'

'I wouldn't have guessed, Tucker, thank you.'

'Then they got off the motorway and were going down these country lanes, but fast. And the bloke on the back got colder and colder.'

'I say, poor chap. Listen Tucker, my Dad's waiting outside with the van.'

'You're spoiling it Alan. This bloke's hands got so numb he lost his grip and fell off at a roundabout. Suddenly the biker notices he's on his own.'

'Very intelligent bloke that. What was he riding – a Honda?'

'Shut up. He turns back and goes up to the roundabout. There's a crowd all round something that's lying on the ground. He races up and says, 'That's my mate, is he all right?''

'And they said, 'No, he's broken his neck'?'

'No, they said. "Yes, he's O.K. His head was twisted round at first, but we've got it the right way round now."'

'Thank you, Tucker, and what else do you do? May I go and do some work now, or . . .'

'Your trouble is you're just miserable, Alan, because you're downtrodden, a mere wage slave . . .'

'I don't know about the wage, Tucker . . .'

'When you could be a member of a self-help group.'

'Self-what group? I thought that was something boys weren't supposed to do.'

'Self help group, you get together with your mates and do things.'

'Like I said, boys aren't supposed to . . .'

'Repair bikes, do car jobs. You get help from the council. You keep the dole but you can earn up to five quid a week each – if you put one in to the kitty for admin.'

'Tucker, the last time I put something in a kitty with you, it was a disaster area. Never again, I said, never again I mean. Besides, five quid a week for all that hassle.'

'It's more than you are getting from your papa, Humphreys.'

'You could be right there. Look, I've got to go.'

'Let's talk about it, mate.'

'Let's talk, but not about it. I don't want to know, Tucker.'

'You'll be sorry.'

Tucker spent the afternoon trying to find Tommy, but was told he'd gone working with a mate of his Dad, window cleaning. That figured. He realised that he was not going to get his self-help group off the ground immediately.

He rang Terry at the Careers Office.

'Hello, Peter. Glad you rang. We've something in the paint and deco line.'

'Yeah?'

'Labouring. Small firm. They just want a reliable lad. £1.50 an hour, but it sounds as though you'll have to work for it. Shall I give you the address?'

'O.K.,' said Tucker.

Day Eighteen

Tucker managed to get on the road by eight o'clock the next morning. The day was fine but cold and he felt it as he started the bike and got on to the road. He'd managed some weeks before to fit himself up from top to toe, with helmet and boots, but the bit in between was more difficult. What he wanted was a Belstaff, but that was going to cost him . . . fifty notes. Still, at £1.50 an hour, who knew, maybe, by the end of the month . . .

Walkers Yard, his new job location, wasn't far. In fact it

was about half a mile past the site where Roller and his gang worked. He shot a quick glance through the padlocked gate as he went past, but the place was empty and the hut closed up. They must use it just when they were doing a job. Maybe he could nip down there at weekends. Worth a try.

'You're late.'

As he drove into the yard and pulled up, he was greeted by an enormously fat man with a filthy trilby topping his red face. This must be 'Mr Walker'.

'Get yourself overalls out of the shed. You're going out on a job with Harry. Put your bike over by the fence.'

'Won't I need it?'

'No, go in the van.'

'Don't you want my . . .?'

'Bugger that, squire. Get moving. Harry's been waiting half the morning as it is.'

Harry, a little man with a large purple nose, smiled amiably at Tucker from the cab of the van, which was already loaded with planks, brushes and cans of paint. Tucker, bursting out of a suit of overalls made for a five year old, climbed into the cab, a few minutes later, Harry said, as he started the engine: – 'Take no notice of the gaffer, son. This is a three day job, you don't even have to come into the yard in the morning. Out of sight, out of mind. You'll be all right with Harry.'

'Where are we going?' asked Tucker, as the van wheezed its way out of the yard.

'Oh, half a mile down the road to the underpass at the junction.'

'What are we doing, then?'

'Doing? We're doing the underpass, that's what.'

Harry said no more, but five minutes later, pulled off the road, ran down a side slope and parked in the shadow of the concrete wall beneath the main road.

61

'There y'are. Get the cans of white off the back. That's all we need for now.'

'What're we doing?'

'I told you. The underpass. You'll see.'

Tucker saw, as they passed into the dark square entrance of the underpass. He smelt it, too, an all-over aroma of damp and cat piss. Ahead of them, some sixty or seventy yards to the other side of the road, some ten feet high on either side, stretched the underpass wall. Tucker saw all right.

From end to end every square foot of the rough concrete surface was covered in graffiti.

'We're going to paint *that*?'

'We are. Contract for the council. Forth Bridge job.'

'You're kidding. What's the point? If we paint it white, they'll come along and do black lettering on it.'

'S'right, son. Then we come back and do it over in black. Like I told you, it's a Forth Bridge job.'

He stopped by the entrance and dropped the brushes.

'Look, start here and work your way forward, go as high as you can without straining anything. We'll do the top later on. Thing is, make a start. Slap it on as thick as you like. Main thing is to cover up the naughty words so the Mothers' Union people can't see 'em when they come past. Off you go, lad. This is work of social importance, not like the rubbish they usually give to school leavers.'

'What about you?'

'I'm going to fix something. Shan't be long.'

Tucker got to work. He soon got into the swing of it, worked too fast at first, but gradually slowed down to ease the ache that crept into his shoulders. He found himself working out how much he had done and how much he should do before they knocked off for the day. Three day job, Harry reckoned. he couldn't see it, with two of them. But he soon did.

Half an hour later Harry re-appeared with a mug and a

thermos. No sooner had he given Tucker his mug of tea, when he vanished.

In fact, Tucker never saw him again. He worked on more slowly, edging his way into the main body of the artistic work on the wall.

'Mandy is a wind surfer. She does it standing up.'

He whited that out regretfully.

'Shane P_____ is bent. It is true.'

That could be libellous. He whited that out and hoped Shane whoever-he-was, would be grateful.

'Jacko is a pillock,' Dogger has a ten inch . . .' whatever it was, Tucker censored it. He paused for breath. His arm was getting tired. He changed arms and worked on for a bit. If Harry'd come back he could go and get himself a snack. He'd forgotten to bring anything with him. But there was no sign of Harry. If he didn't get back by lunch. Tucker'd have to leave the stuff on the van and eat . . .

Half past eleven. He was getting bored. He'd done about twenty yards, he reckoned. No wonder it was a three day job. He'd give it half an hour more, then break. He began to amuse himself by adding comments to some of the slogans.

Under 'Sniper and Bullet', he wrote 'Wank and Blank'. 'Steve has all my heart – Karen.' he added: 'Don't trust him Karen, he's two timing you with Sandra.'

Suddenly a slogan, large and crudely daubed, letters a foot high 'Abandon Wog . . .' It became cruder as it went along trailing away into obscenities towards the other end of the underpass. He dug his brush into the can and began to walk along the slogan drawing a broad band of white across it. His brush ran out near the end and he walked back to re-charge.

Just as he bent over the bucket, a slight noise warned him someone was behind him. He turned. There were three of them. And two he recognised right away from the bundle in

63

the Careers Office the week before. One was Booga Benson, the second his mate. The other he didn't know, but didn't want to. Booga spoke:

'What do you think you're doing?'

Tucker said nothing. Booga went on: 'It took a lot of trouble painting that on the wall. And you are now going to get some different colour paint from your little van and put our nice slogan back just how it was.'

One of the three moved behind him. He was trapped.

Tucker moved forward, between Booga and his mate. They were taken off balance. They'd expected him to try and run the other way. With a quick double swing of his arm, to left and right, he swept his brush first across Booga's face, then across the other's ugly mug. It must have improved them no end, but he did not wait to admire his own handiwork.

Flinging the brush behind him, he raced down the under-pass, up the slope and past the van. Where the hell was Harry when he needed him? He heard their boots thumping down in the passage behind him as he flung himself at the wall at the top of the slope.

They were coming up the rise as he made his third attempt, his fingers caught the top of the wall. With a great heave that cracked his shoulder muscles, he drew himself up, rolled over and dropped with a bone-jarring crash onto the pavement between two ladies with shopping baskets. He didn't wait to hear what they had to say, because a quick glance back told him his pursuers were walking up the wall on the other side.

He dodged into a side street, back round to the other side of the junction and nipped smartly into the gents to remove his overalls. With these safely rolled up under his arm, he strolled gently back to the yard to report to Mr Walker.

Mr Walker was already waiting for him.

'You're fired.'

'But, I was . . .'

'Don't waste my time. I know what you were doing. I've just had some people on the phone about it.'

'But you can't give me the push without notice. It's against the law,' protested Tucker.

'Don't give me the flaming law. I'll tell you what the law is. Up to four weeks I can sack you on the spot and I'm doing it.'

Tucker stood his ground: 'I want my pay. I did three hours work.'

'I'll give you two quid and think yourself lucky. I'm deducting for damage. Brushes lost, cans of paint thrown all over the place. Two quid. Take it or leave it.'

Tucker began to protest. Walker said: 'On your bike, squire.'

And that was that. The worst thing was, the bike wouldn't start.

Day Nineteen

As he strolled into the Employment Office Tucker saw the tall dark girl on her way out. She looked away, a bit too quickly, he thought. Must be playing hard to get. He concentrated his attention on the clerk at Box Six.

To his surprise she greeted him pleasantly. There was no mention of his having taken and lost a job, for the princely sum of £1.50. Then he remembered, as he took his attendance card out of his pocket, that he'd forgotten to post his Parts 2 and 3. There were some advantages in being absent minded. He leaned on the counter.

'With this new job-sharing lark, we could split it, if you like. I mean I could sit behind the desk and sign you on the first half of the week, and you could sit behind and sign me on the second half.'

She gazed at him coolly, though not unfriendly. He made a quick gorilla face at her. Her mouth twitched slightly.

'Next please.'

A visit to the Job Centre and then to the Careers Office yielded nothing. Terry, he was relieved, took it very calmly when he revealed he'd lost the job at Walker's. Terry confirmed that Walker was within his rights in sacking him on the spot: 'You get notice only after you've worked for four weeks, Peter.'

Tucker grunted: 'I don't know, this whole system's full of Catch 22's isn't it? You get no experience without a job, but you don't get any job without experience. And when you get a job they sack you without notice before you've got time to have any rights.'

'You'll have to keep trying, Peter.'

Keep trying? But not any more today, he decided. There was a limit to the kicks you could get out of banging your head on a wall.

On impulse he got out his bike and rode round to the site. It might be that Roller's mob had finished their work and had cleared off, in which case he could have the place to himself.

But as he paused at the top of the slope he could see they were still in occupation. The gate was open and the grey truck was down by the hut. Roller and his team were standing round looking at something.

While he rested there, engine idling, he heard a shout and Roller broke free from the group and came scouring up the ramp towards him at a tremendous rate. Tucker made ready to push off rapidly when he saw that Roller was signalling for him to stop.

'Hang about, friend, hang about. We need your... expert advice.'

Tucker looked at Roller as he coasted gently round him wheels buzzing.

'What on?' he asked suspiciously.

Roller jerked his head towards the truck at the foot of the slope.

'Some idiot with a bike we picked up along the road. Says it won't go. We can't see anything wrong, but we don't know bikes.'

Tucker grinned: 'What's in it for me?'

Roller grinned back: 'What we get out of him, less . . .' he left the sentence unfinished. 'You coming?'

Tucker followed him down to the shed. The group broke apart as they pulled up. Standing in their midst was a thin individual with a petulant face, dressed in a one piece leather zipper fronted with 'Team Yamaha'. Tucker gave him one look. He guessed that on the back of that expensive outfit would be Number 7, a Barry Sheene freak.

Roller was right. This was an idiot. His glance turned to the machine, a Honda Silver Wing, the half litre version. A rich idiot.

'Here you are – sir,' said Roller, 'our motor cycle mechanic.'

The young bloke looked at Tucker and his machine. Tucker could see the wheels going round inside that head.

'Let's have a look,' he said.

'It was making this awful offbeat noise, you know. No power at all. But for heaven's sake, it's a new machine.'

'Not to say it can't go wrong,' said Tucker. He walked to the other side of the bike. He almost burst out laughing. So that was what it was.

'Look it's,' he began, when he caught Roller's eye. There was just the suspicion of a head-shake and a flicker of the eye-lid.

'It's going to take a little while, I think.'

'Oh,' fretted the youth, 'how long? I'm due at my girl friend's at five.'

'Well, half an hour, maybe, an hour. Not much more.' He looked at Roller. Roller placed a fatherly hand on the client's arm. 'Don't worry, sir. Our man's sh--, first rate. Why don't you go up to the cafe on the main road there, have a cup of coffee and come back at 3.15.'

As they watched the leather suited figure disappear up the ramp, Roller punched Tucker good naturedly.

'You are learning. Now tell us what's wrong?'

Tucker beckoned. Roller, Hughes and the others came round the machine. He pointed: 'The plug cap's come off and the H.T. lead's hanging there, earthing out behind the right hand cylinder.'

'So?'

'So, if you've got a spare, we can screw it on. Just like that!'

Tucker straddled the machine, started the engine and took it gently round the concrete apron.

He speeded up, feeling the power beneath him. This was a beauty. It was Concorde compared with his own bike, which was inside the legal 125 limit. For a moment he felt envious. He rode it round a few times more, then took it back to the shed.

Roller gestured with his thumb. Tucker looked up – the zipper suit boy was coming back.

'Customer's anxious. Shall I make him hang about some more, friend?'

'Nah,' said Tucker, 'let him have it.'

The young man was excited: 'That's awfully quick. And I could see from the road, it's going like a bomb.' He looked at Tucker: 'How much?'

Tucker started to speak when Roller interrupted smoothly: 'Strictly speaking we should charge a minimum hour's labour, sir, which is £10, plus parts, transport and so on, around £15. But,' he half glanced at Tucker, 'we'll make it £8.'

'Oh, I say, that is reasonable. What was wrong?'

'Just some adjustments on your right hand cylinder,' said Tucker. He couldn't manage the 'sir' but, he hadn't Roller's style.

As the young man drove off, Tucker turned to Roller who held the notes in his hand.

'That's five for you, friend, three for us.'

'Eh!'

'Three, man. One for transport, one for rent of garage space, and – one for instruction in sales technique.'

He pushed Tucker lightly: 'You aim to start in the repair business. You need to start training, now.'

Day Twenty

Tucker sat in the caff. His brother was back in town from the oil rig. He hadn't reported home yet – shacked up somewhere else, no doubt. But there was a half promise to meet up for a chat, and Tucker was rather looking forward to swapping a few yarns, about the great world of work.

While he drank his coffee, he did his accounts. And they were looking rather good. In the kitty was £14.35. And that was £2.40 up on the beginning of the week. The first time he'd shown a profit. And a few more idiots on Honda Silver Wings with a screw loose and he'd be home and dry. What's more he was only half way to the deadline. Things were looking good.

It was at that moment that a shadow fell over his hopes for the future. In fact a shadow fell over his coffee cup and his piece of paper. Someone was standing against th table, pressing it against him. And since he was sitting with his back to the wall, it was distinctly uncomfortable.

'Knock it off,' he said, looking up.

Booga Benson and his mates stood there, grinning. They were glad to see him, it seemed. He wasn't glad to see them. Even if they had scrubbed the paint off their faces. That must have been the first wash they'd had since that rainy period in July.

Booga leaned forward. The table was slowly cutting Tucker in half.

Booga had a look on his face as though he had been thinking and was pleased with himself over it.

'First the good news, Jenkins. The good news is that you get a warning. You and your little wog mechanics did something naughty. You picked up a geezer with a bike on one of our streets.'

'I didn't pick anybody up,' said Tucker, but said no more as another shove on the table top cut off his breath.

'We are not asking, we are telling,' said Benson. There was an air about him. They must have been educating him in that remand centre. There was less of the gorilla and more of the chimpanzee about him. He didn't need anybody to wind him up and point him any more. He could think out nasties and do them on his own. Tucker braced his hands against the table top. If he could only get some leverage, he'd wait for the right moment and shove the lot over. He looked over at the counter, but the bloke by the coffee machine was not noticing anything today.

'Now that's your warning. Don't do it again on our patch. That's what you don't do. Now we come to what you did do. And you did something we didn't like twice, didn't you?'

Another sickening lunge on the table.

'So for that we are going to bust you – again. You didn't like it last time, did you? This time is going to make that like a lovely memory. But we don't want blood on the crockery do we so we're taking you round the back, where we can put some time in without interference.'

70

Tucker braced himself again as they leaned forward.

Behind them the door of the cafe opened. Booga and his men turned round. In the doorway stood Paddy and Tucker's brother. Each on their own they were big. Together they looked horrible.

'Hello, Peter,' said Paddy, coming forward to the table.

Benson made the connection and moved rapidly for the door, followed by his mates. But Tucker's brother stopped them in their tracks. 'Somebody was making promises,' he said. 'People who do that should be able to carry them out. I don't think you can.'

He raised his hand and took Booga's nose gently between his fingers.

As he massaged it slowly, he said, with equal slowness. 'Now if you do anything like you just said you were going to do, I shall pull off your arms and hit you with the wet end.'

He released Booga, and opened the door: 'On your way. And remember, if I'm not here, my mate will be and what he'll do to you will be so bad you'll beg for me to come back and take over.'

Booga and his men vanished. Paddy and Tucker's brother sat down.

'What was that all about?' he asked.

He told them. His brother shook his head.

'You want to watch it mate. The re-spray trade's very dodgy – dotty number plates and all that. This Roller's mob. Are they clean?'

'Yeah,' said Tucker, 'I'm sure. Sure as I'm sure Benson isn't'

Paddy leaned forward: 'Peter. What happened to you outside the Labour that day? I got held up inside. One of the boys wanted my advice. When I got out the law had taken my leaflets and you were away across the road with a gent with a brief case. I decided not to follow you in case it was private.'

'I wish you had, Paddy.' He told the story of Barraclough and his con-trick.

'What a rip off,' said his brother, 'and doing it with kids on the dole. He wants his arm bending the wrong way, he does.'

'Anyway, Peter, accept my apologies. Let me get you a cup of coffee.'

While Paddy was at the counter, Tucker's brother said quickly, 'Listen, mate. Have you got any cash on you?'

'Yeah,' said Tucker, 'Why?'

'Lend us five will you – I mean, if you can. Paddy's broke. There's a bloke I'm meeting tonight who owes me. We're having a poker school. I'm coming round home, tomorrow night, just to look in, you know. I'll let you have it back then, with divi.'

His voice lowered: 'Tell you what, let's have another five if you've got it. I'll put it in for you. I could double it easy. You get the same on yours that I get on mine. O.K.?'

Tucker thought for a moment. Their kid was mad, but he was O.K.

He handed over the second five. Paddy loomed over him.

'You're not lending this character money, are you, Peter? You shouldn't, you know.' He turned to Tucker's brother: 'You've no business, you know, Jenks.'

'Ah, s'all right, Paddy,' said Tucker. He could look after himself.

'I hope so,' said Paddy as if he read Tucker's thoughts.

Day Twenty-One

Sunday. Day of Rest. Tucker slept in until lunch time.

In the afternoon, he met Alan and Tommy. Tommy was in good spirits. He'd done a week's window cleaning and was flush. Off and on he had been seeing the blonde girl he'd met in the pub. It had to be more off than on because of the size of her boy friend.

'You like living dangerously, don't you Watson?' said Tucker. 'Just don't count on us bailing you out every time, though. One day, somebody'll catch up with you and all we may be able to do is come to the funeral.'

Tommy grinned: 'If I worried about things like that, you can come to my funeral tomorrow.'

'Anyway,' he added, 'old Humphreys looks as though he's attending his own funeral.'

'That's true, you're looking distinctly down in the mouth and grey round the edges, Alan,' said Tucker. 'What's up? Tell Uncle.'

Alan shrugged.

'Let's guess. Three Guesses. Miss MacMahon, Miss MacMahon or Miss MacMahon. Which is it?'

'You cheated,' said Tommy, 'you looked.'

'Why don't you two funny men just get lost?' muttered Alan.

'Sorry mate,' said Tucker, seriously. 'But you are an old misery guts just lately. What's she been on about?'

'I know what it is,' he went on. 'She's been trying to get him to go to college with her. And he's weakening.'

'Mind you,' said Tommy, 'he could be better off there than supporting the family business. That's not doing him any good, either.'

Taking the bull by the horns, Tucker said: 'Look Alan, old son, why don't you just give her the bullet? There's no future in it. You don't go with a bird to make yourself miserable, now, do you? I know you were childhood sweethearts and all that, but maybe she wants to play with other boys. She's just nagging you about college to make you feel inferior.'

'Listen, mate, I'll . . .' Alan suddenly turned on Tucker.

'Hey, hey, gents,' intervened Tommy hastily, 'no bloodshed, please. Look, let's go and have a drink. I'll pay,' he added.

'You've convinced me,' said Tucker. 'Come on, Alan.' He put his arm on his mate's shoulder. 'Forget I said anything.'

When Tucker got home in the evening, his parents were out. As he sat watching the box with a can from the fridge, the phone rang. It was his brother.

'Listen, mate. Can you let them know I can't get home tonight. I'm otherwise engaged. I'll be calling in sometime in the week.'

'Hey, O.K. How did it go last night?' asked Tucker.

'What go? Oh, that. Christ, mate. Disaster from the word go. Every wrong card in the pack. Look, I'll let you have that ten before I go back. No sweat, mate.'

No sweat? Speak for yourself, mate.

Day Twenty-Two

Loose end day. Alan's Dad was away for several days and Alan was unemployed as well as on the dole. Tommy's window cleaning job had gone, he'd been displaced by a needy member of the window cleaner's family.

Neither showed much enthusiasm for Tucker's idea of teaming up to repair bikes. And as Tucker realised, that idea needed funds. Which he had not. At the last count he had £2.35 to last until the next green and white cheque. He had assets, of course, he had £10 out on loan to his brother, which might yield a dividend. On the other hand, he had to admit that it was high risk capital. Paddy was right, he shouldn't have lent it, but turning his brother down didn't appeal to him either. So he had cash flow problems.

They stood on the pavement outside the Arndale.

'What do we do today?' asked Alan. He looked at Tucker. 'What does it say in the book?'

Tucker ticked off on his fingers.

'Job Centre?'

'Nah,' said the other two.

'Careers Office?'

'Nah,'

'Go camping?'

'Gertcher'

'Water the pot plants?'

'I'll water you, mate.'

'O.K.,' said Tucker, 'it's two weeks since we looked in the adverts. Let's do the library.'

The others followed reluctantly, but once in the reading room, they quickly got to work, each picking a newspaper and flipping the pages. This time, they were alone in the room.

'Here we are,' called Tommy. '£1800 a month, car owner, well dressed, intelligent, dedicated, willing to start immediately.'

'Here's a better one, doorkeeper, impeccably. mannered, mature.'

'How much?'

'Six thousand a year.'

'Stupid. They could board it up for twenty quid.'

'Hey, listen to this – Chauffeur, send references, curriculum vitae and snapshot. What's curriculum vitae?'

'Ah, it just means what other work you've done.'

'Why can't they just say that?'

'Ah, that's it, you get a different class of person that way.'

'Stupid, I reckon.'

'That rules you out right away, mate. Here you are 'Life Drawing Models' – must not get students too worked up.'

'It doesn't say that, you berk.'

'I know it doesn't, but I could write better adverts myself.'

'Pull the other,' said Alan.

'O.K.,' said Tucker, 'How's this – The Times.' He altered his voice: 'Mother's help. Au pair to look after Katrina and Fiona while Mama has it away with local television producer.'

'Right,' said Alan, 'Sun – 'Universal Grinder.' Must have good track record. Heavy breathers not wanted.'

Tommy had moved away to another reading stand and was turning the pages of the Guardian.

'See this,' he called. 'you can stop worrying about unemployment. It says here working class youth adapt fairly well to being out of work. Unemployment is most distressing for middle class school leavers who come from a group accustomed to well paid and satisfying employment.'

'What's all that supposed to mean?'

'Simple, isn't it? It means you're thick so you don't feel anything, doesn't it?'

'The crap some of these geezers write. You know, I heard a talk on the radio the other day. This bloke reckons that millions are never going to work again and the best they can do is learn to use their leisure time.'

'Lie back and enjoy it, eh?'

'O.K., if you're loaded. If you're not it gets on your tit, doesn't it.'

'Talking about being loaded, who's paying for coffee?'

'Dunno.'

'Tell you what. Last one there pays.'

They crashed through the doors almost bowling over the young librarian they'd met before.

His mouth was open as though he was going to give them his 'keep the noise down' routine.

Tucker stopped a second, to take him by the arm: 'Sorry, can't stay to talk. Urgent appointment.'

They rushed out on to the street, laughing pushing and shoving. The librarian took a deep breath and went back to his work.

Day Twenty-Three

Tucker sat on the park bench. It was a fine day, mild and sunny. September was nearly over and he was almost broke again. He watched the leaves falling from the trees. Some fluttered right down. Some seemed to take their time. He found himself watching one particular leaf hanging on by a thread and speculating when it would fall. He tried to remember what he learnt in science about the rate of gravity, and found his mind was almost blank. All that time spent learning something and not a trace of it.

Then he caught sight of Alan and Tommy across by the rec. ground, left his seat and set off at a run. They broke into a run as well and all three headed for the kids' swings. There were only two. Tucker and Alan grabbed them, while Tommy contented himself with leaping on to the iron tubing at the top of the frame and sending out wild ape cries.

'Do you mind? Honestly, you'd think people had better things to do. Like big kids.'

Two young women with small children stood behind them.

Embarrassed Tucker and Alan shoved off the swing seats and moved away. Tommy remained behind and as Tucker looked back, he saw Tommy pushing one of the kids in the swing. Then he noticed one of the women was a blonde.

'Hey,' he said to Alan, as they crossed the road to the caff, 'does that bird of Tommy's have a kid, then?'

Alan shrugged: 'Tommy's an idiot. Her boy friend is going to catch up with him one day. He's stupid. He'll get his legs busted.'

'I know he's a silly boy. But he keeps cheerful. That's more than I can say for you, old son.'

They sat down in the caff. Alan stirred his coffee.

'Ah, it's not what you're thinking. I'm just bored. I suppose it's because I don't really have to worry. The old man expects me to take over eventually. But I get bored helping him then I get bored not doing anything when he's not there.'

'If that's the way you feel, mate, perhaps you'd be better off taking Susi's advice and going to college.'

'That's it. Only I think I'd feel out of place there. I've seen some of the blokes and I don't fancy spending my time in their company.'

'Well, there's no satisfying some people. If sex, work, education, business have all let you down, what are you going to do to pass the time? What's it to be, booze, grass, magic mushrooms or half a yard of glue up your hooter?'

Alan stared at Tucker. 'Don't talk stupid. Mind you there's a bloke down our road, he's been out of work for a year. He's on the bottle most of the time. You see him down the road sometimes, paralytic. But he never gets picked up. But if he had just one smoke, the Law would be on to him like a shot.'

'There's no justice. Here's Tommy. Right, Tommy lad, you're paying.'

'What d'you mean?'

'You were last in, right?'

'That was yesterday.'

'And what's the difference?'

Day Twenty-Four

In the morning Tucker went through the card, mechanically and without any result – Job Centre, Careers Office. He even went to the Library again, quietly, and noted one or two jobs.

Back home he pondered what to do.

He could sit down and write some letters asking for jobs. It didn't appeal to him, frankly, crawling to people he didn't know, who didn't want to know him.

Or he could do what was in the back of his mind. Put an ad in the local paper, offering to repair bikes. If he got any jobs, he could use Roller's place – at the usual rates. There was Booga Benson in the woodwork, of course. But that was probably all mouth. And anyway, if you worried about all the aggro you could get, you'd never go outside the door.

He stolled down to the local paper office. He was running low on petrol. Inside, in reception, he explained what he wanted to the girl there and she went to get the rate card. While they chatted a tall bearded man came in and paused for a moment as though listening. Then he interrupted: 'Excuse me a second. I couldn't help overhearing what you were saying. Could you come through into the editorial? You can sort the ad out afterwards. That is if you have the time?'

The time? One thing Tucker had plenty of was time.

In the larger room beyond, people were busy at desks, typing, chatting, passing bits of paper to and fro. The man came straight to the point.

'Look, I'm doing a feature on the young unemployed. How they manage. The way they go about coping with their situation. Would you like to help?'

Tucker hesitated.

'Look, you give us an interview – in depth thing, the real details, not just a general moan – and we'll arrange a free insert of your ad for four weeks. We can even give you a puff in the article. What do you say?'

That began to sound interesting to Tucker. He was about to sit down when the reporter said: 'Oh sod this, I need a drink. Look, let's go over to the pub and have a ploughman's or scampi and chips or some rubbish like that and a pint. We can talk at our ease.'

That sounded even more interesting.

'O.K.,' said Tucker.

The pub was slowly filling up with lunchtime trade when they entered and approached the bar. The reporter began to order. The barmaid, an attractive slim girl with short curled hair, reached for the pad and pencil and faced them across the bar. She stared at the reporter, then deliberately ignored him and turned to Tucker. She blinked, stared again then grinned: 'Hello. Long time no see.'

Now he stared. It was Trisha Yates.

'Hey, I didn't recognise you without your bonce boppers on.'

She shook her head: 'You don't change, do you, Jenkins?'

'My apologies. Force of habit. But I didn't recognise you with the new hair do.'

'Yeah, 'tis a bit drastic but I wanted a change. Like it?'

'It's great.'

'Anyway, what are you having?'

Tucker turned. 'This gent's ordering.' But the reporter had vanished.

'He must have gone to the gents,' he said.

Trisha shook her head. 'No he didn't. He walked right out. And a good job too, because I wouldn't have served him – not even if I got the sack for it.'

'Hey, why not?'

'Look, Peter, I can't really stop to chat now. Let me get you something now and maybe we can have a chat for five minutes when things get slack.'

'When do you finish?'

'Two thirty. I only do two hours twice a week. Daren't do any more.'

'Tell you what, when you've finished, let's go to the caff.'

'Oh, will you wait? You don't mind?' She looked surprised.

He shook his head. They grinned at one another. He took his drink and sat down to wait.

Shortly before closing time she came over to where he was sitting, pulling on her jacket. He watched as she approached him. Yates had a terrific figure. She sat down across the table from him. The seats around them were emptying the noise growing less as people went back to work.

'Thanks for waiting,' she said.

'Who's going anywhere?' he asked.

'Like that? This is the first job I've had. What have you been doing – when you're not signing on I mean?'

'Listen, before all that, what happened to that bloke from the paper? Why did he take off like that?'

'Didn't you recognise him?'

'Didn't even recognise you, did I?'

'That was Mr Jeremy Bleeding Hart, that was. Remember? He was the bloke that did that series about

81

school, all the dirt he could throw. After he'd conned me into telling him all the trade secrets.'

'He didn't have a beard though, did he?'

'If he'd had a false nose and a wig, I'd have known him. I'd have smelt him.'

'He really got to you, didn't he – ?' he hesitated.

She laughed: 'You can't think of what to call me can you?'

'You didn't have any trouble at school, did you? Pongo wasn't it?'

'That was a long time ago, I've got more mature tastes now.'

'Thanks, whatever it means. Anyway what did Hart want with you?'

'He was going to do an interview about how the young unemployed cope.'

'I bet he was. You know what it'd be. Young Britain on the fiddle. It'd be a knocking piece. He just can't help ripping people off.'

'You still sound bitter, Trish.'

She coloured slightly: Well, I am. I hate people who tell lies anyway. But he – ' she stopped. 'I suppose I'm really angry at being taken in.'

'Easy enough.' He thought a second, then told her about Barraclough and the bottle-depot fiddle. She didn't laugh.

'I hate people like that, I'd string 'em up.' She looked at him again. 'Anyway what have you been up to?'

'Mostly trying to get out of being shipped off back to school.'

She shook her head. 'Incredible, isn't it? I wouldn't mind, but they won't hear of it. So what I'm doing is drawing the dole, doing this part time job, and going to college. Provided I don't earn more than £4 a week and don't go to college more than twenty-one hours, I'm O.K.'

'That's crazy. They stop your dole if you study too much?

How are you supposed to qualify for anything? They won't give you a job unless you've got qualifications. They stop your dole if you try and get 'em. They're a bunch of sadists.'

'Well, they reckon that those who go back to school anyway don't get any dole. That's why my Mum won't have me studying full time. We can't afford it, she reckons. And she reckons it's a waste of time girls going in for higher education.'

'Well, if they're only going to get married and have kids.'

'Oh, don't you start, Peter. There's one or two of the girls I know have just got pregnant and are staying at home. They reckon there's nothing better to do than have a baby.'

'Well, there is nothing better to do than . . .'

'You blokes are all the same, aren't you?'

'Since when did you join Women's Lib?'

'You're joking. Seriously though, I suppose I've been the same since I was a kid. I didn't see why I shouldn't do the things I wanted just because I was a girl.'

'What's your mate Hargreaves doing?'

'Cathy? Oh she's a right idiot. She's still messing about with that group. And just to keep in touch she works in this music shop. And she's let the manager con her into doing two days a week 'voluntary', running a fan club. It's a right fiddle. They let you earn extra money, provided it goes to voluntary activities. So in fact she's really working in the shop and he pays her 50p an hour on the side.'

'It's a rip off. Why doesn't she just walk out?'

'Because there's plenty other little girls who'd walk right in. And anyway, she reckons she meets pop musicians and other people this way. Could be right. But she's still being used.'

'Dead right. Listen, Trish, what are you studying?'

'I want to get on the graphics course, design work. One girl I know got a great job in a record company designing sleeves. But the course is full up, and I need maths first anyway.'

'So you weren't joking about that row you kicked up over technical drawing at school, then?' asked Tucker.

She shook her head.

'I just kicked up then because I thought I had a right. Since then I've got really interested. I'm going to do something.'

'I bet you are.'

'You taking the mick, Jenkins?'

'A bit, but not much.'

She jumped up. 'Hey, I've got to dash. I've got lectures in half an hour.'

She put a hand on his sleeve. 'It was great seeing you, Peter.'

They stood together on the pavement outside.

'Do you ever miss those times we had at school?'

He grinned. 'Once a week, maybe, when I'm out of my skull with boredom.'

She turned and ran.

'See you,' she called. She pointed towards the pub, 'Tuesday lunch, Thursday evenings.'

'See you.'

Day Twenty-Five

Tucker rode down to Roller's place. The gate was padlocked, the area empty. That was the second time. Had something happened? Had they been frightened off? Or closed down? Or gone bust? Anything could happen.

He ran the bike round half a dozen times. He was running low on petrol. Then he drove up to the Job Centre. It was empty and he spent ten minutes looking round the cards, without finding a job that even looked like him.

He was just about to go again, when someone spoke to him. A man was at his side, biggish, pale faced. In fact to Tucker he looked as sick as a parrot. He whispered: 'Is this where you sign on?'

Tucker started to say, 'No, mate you want the Labour in . . .' when he remembered his own first day.

'Is it a new claim?'

The man looked blank.

'I mean, is it the first time you're out of work.'

His voice rose, in reply: 'First time in my whole bloody life. You know, they told me if I went on permanent nights, they'd keep me on, then, they closed the whole department, the lot. No notice. Just like that.'

His voice wavered. He was shattered.

'Look,' said Tucker. 'Ask at the desk. They'll tell you. You may have to go to the Labour anyway, and you'll have to go to the Social Security as well.'

'I don't want social security.'

'Listen mate, if you're entitled to it, you take it. There's plenty doing it.'

'O.K., er , thanks.'

'Good luck, mate.'

'Thanks.'

As the man walked away, Tucker knew where he'd seen him before. It was the character in pyjamas who'd shouted at him when he was runnng the bike along the backs.

But now he looked younger.

Or maybe Tucker felt older.

Day Twenty-Six

Signing on.

No sign of the tall girl with dark hair.

But someone else was very friendly.

'Hello.'

He looked at the girl behind the counter. She smiled.

'It wouldn't work, you know.'

'What wouldn't?' he was baffled.

'You suggested sharing my job.'

'Yeah, I did, what's wrong with it?'

'Promotion. Blokes have three times as much chance as women of making supervisor. Who's chance do we have, yours or mine?'

'I'll think that one over.'

'Bye.'

'Bye.'

'Next please.'

Day Twenty-Seven

Another weekend, another month. Tucker had high hopes of both the £250,000 prize and the £100,000 prize from his Premium Bond. But as it happened, nothing came.

So he had a quid to last him until Monday when the giro cheque should come, and ten quid invested in his fly-by-night brother, who might be back on his oil rig off the Shetlands for all he knew.

In just four weeks, what had he done? He'd earned nearly twenty, which was more or less the amount he'd lost.

His dole money had gone keeping himself and his bike on the road. In fact both were just about roadworthy, but how long could it last? He'd been lucky so far having no clothes to buy.

He'd done all he could, he had to admit that, but the net result was he was no further forward than when he started, except for what he'd learnt about life on the dole. And he had less than two weeks to come up with something to convince his Dad he didn't need to go back to school.

Why should he give himself brain damage over it? Why not go back for a year?

The thought of it got him to his feet and took him round to Alan's. By the time he had Alan on his feet and picked up Tommy it was nearly lunch time. They stood on the corner by the pub.

'Going in?'

'Who's paying?'

'Last one up to the bar.'

The three of them arrived in a dead heat. Tucker stared. Trisha was behind the bar.

'I thought you said "Tuesdays and Thursdays"'.

'I did. I'm just doing them a favour.'

'Doesn't that take you over the earnings limit?'

'It does. I'm doing myself a favour this week.'

'Say no more.' He turned to Alan and Tommy.

'This is a lady I used to know at school.'

'That's not what you said when you were at school, you pig,' said Alan. 'How's it going, Trish?' he added.

'Fine. How's Susi?'

'Great,' said Alan.

An uneasy silence followed. Tucker broke in: 'We'll have a pint of Guinness and three straws, Trish.'

'Like that, eh? Listen, have one on me – and the DHSS' They looked at each other.

'And why not. Are you celebrating?'

'As a matter of fact I am,' said Trisha.

What, you got a job?'

She shook her head.

'Better. Tutor at college is going to bend the rules so I can get on the graphics course right away. Take my maths at the same time. Comes to twenty hours altogether, so I keep inside the dole limit. Only thing is, if I get offered a job, I have to pull out of the course.'

'Stupid, isn't it? Anyway, Trish, good luck.'

They drank, then moved away to a table. After a while, Tucker on a trip to the gents paused at the bar.

'Going anywhere after you've finished?' he asked casually.

She looked awkward, 'I am – sorry.'

'See you.'

'See you.'

Day Twenty-Eight

The holy peace of Tucker's Sunday lie-in was shattered when his mother called him.

'There's someone on the phone, Peter.'

'If it's Alan I'll call him back next month.'

'No, it's a man, Joe someone or other, I didn't catch it properly.'

Puzzled, Tucker struggled up and staggered to the phone, clutching his pyjama trousers round him. His mother raised her eyebrows and walked away into the kitchen.

'Hello?'

'Peter Jenkins?'

'Yeah?' Who was this?

'You don't know me. My name's Joe Kirman. But I know your brother and I know Paddy Riordan.'

'Oh, yeah, right.'

'Paddy tells me you're looking for work, on bikes.'

Good old Paddy. But what had he let him in for?

'You still there?'

'Sure, Joe. What sort of work are you talking about?'

'Difficult to describe over the phone. But come round to 18 Netherfield Gardens.'

'When shall I come?'

'Well, how about now?'

'I'll be ten minutes.'

He was out of the house and on his bike before his mother had finished saying: 'What about your breakfast, Peter.' Netherfield wasn't all that far away. A terrace of small houses with their front doors right on the pavement. Tucker pulled up left his bike standing and made the single step that brought him up to the knocker of number 18.

He knocked once. He knocked again, louder. No sign. He looked at the door. This was number 18. Was somebody putting him on? He gave the door another bash. Then he noticed another noise. Someone was banging on a window. He looked round. Up, down. He could see nothing. There was the noise again. Then he saw, the lace curtains right by the front door were pushed back. An old woman looked out at him. She made a sign to him that could have been rude. But when she gestured again Tucker realised she was saying: 'Go round the back.'

He ran his bike to the end, round the block and up the dirt road which ran along the back of the houses. Each had a small back yard and garden with a high wooden fence. Which was number 18? he wondered as he chugged along. No numbers. He tried counting but wasn't quite sure.

In the end he killed the motor, left the bike standing against the fence and heaved himself up to look over. At first jump it was too high for him, but he scrabbled with his boots against he timber and got his arms over to look down.

There in front of his fascinated gaze, was a small patch of lawn, and two people, with very little on. She was lying on her back, he was bending over. He seemed to be rubbing something into her skin. Tucker blinked. It was a lovely autumn day, and sunny, but this was amazing. It was incredible what went on.

Suddenly her eyes turned to the fence. She screamed and pushed at the bloke and pointed. Tucker dropped down so hard he knocked the wind out of himself. From the other side of the fence he heard angry voices.

'I'll get my trousers.'

Tucker moved. Without hesitation he lunged for the next door in the fence and pushed against it. Luckily it came open and he shot inside.

This must be number 18. There was no grass, only yard and it was littered with gear in a trail that led up to a small shed with open door revealing more parts, tools, a bike.

In the middle of the yard stood another bike, a Ducatti big, lean and powerful. Behind it, in his shirt sleeves, up to the elbow in the bike's innards like a vet helping a cow give birth was a big bloke. Bigger than Paddy, with blonde hair and beard, streaked with oil and sweat.

He took no notice of Tucker. He was muttering to himself as if praying.

'Now, Number One, Top dead centre Number Two, inlet. No, sod it. Eight of the bastards and... Number One, Top...'

He stopped as the gate behind Tucker burst open, swinging round to conceal him, and a man and woman rushed in. Tucker knew who they were, even dressed.

'Joe. Have you seen a bleeding Peeping Tom? Just looking over our fence. He was one of these...'

Tucker quickly loosened his straps.

'Cyclists,' went on the bloke, 'he had a helmet on.'

Tucker whipped it off as the man turned and saw him.

'Isn't that him, Sandra?'

The woman stared. 'I don't know. He had one of those dark things on his face.'

'Him,' said Joe, without looking up from his valves, 'the only bodywork he's interested in is made by Honda. Besides he's too young to know what you were up to. Whatever it was you were up to.'

'Come on,' said the man, 'I'll have a look down the end.'

The two went out. Tucker drew another breath.

'Shut the gate, mate.'

Joe looked up at Tucker.

'What were you doing?' he asked. 'Never mind.' He looked down at the valves.

'Why do I do people favours? I'll tell you, Joe,' he went on, 'One, because you want your head seeing to. Two, because Paddy's a good man, one of the best, only he's fifty years behind the times.' He looked at Tucker again. 'Not like your brother who is fifty years ahead of the rest of us.'

He got to his feet. 'I used to know Paddy on the building. I do CH now. But I work on my own. I'm fed up of seeing so called businessmen striping up the public. Now *I charge*. But when I put a system in a house, they're right for years.'

He changed tack suddenly.

'How's your brother?'

'Haven't seen him.'

'That figures. Listen Peter. Without giving you my life's story, see that iron in the shed? Right? Yamaha XJ650. Nice machine believe it or not, but about two inches of shit all over it. Don't ask me what the bloke was doing with it, rallying through a treacle factory perhaps. That's for Grace, my lady friend. She was run off the road by some hit and run artist a month ago. If I had his number I'd ram his regi-plates so far up he'd never have tonsilitis again. Anyway, she only had third party so no bike now. So since it's her birthday on the fourteenth, this is her present. When it's cleaned up. I just don't have time. Will you do it?'

Tucker walked up and eyed the machine in the shed. Joe was right. It was covered every inch in black fouling and mud, baked hard.

'O.K.,' he said, thinking at the same time: 'I'm crazy, it's only ten days from now.'

'I'll give you twenty,' said Joe.

Tucker gritted his teeth: 'Twenty-five.'

Joe laughed. 'It had better be brilliant, mate.'

Day Twenty-Nine

No £100,000 premium bond arrived. Not even a £250,000 prize with apologies for late delivery. Even the giro cheque which did come, was a bit frayed round the edges.

They'd deducted his pig farm money, less his £4 earning allowance. So when his Mum's money was put on one side, he had exactly £13.50 in the kitty. That left out the ten quid stake money his brother had. Though Tucker had an increasing feeling he'd be getting that in lubricating oil next time his brother came back from the rig. It was ten days since he'd last seen his brother and in that time there hadn't even been a whisper of him.

Steeling himself, he left £5 in the giro bank and kept back £8.50. That had to see him through the next fortnight, or rather until he finished Joe's bike and got paid. That had to be in ten days time or Joe would pay him off.

So he ran round to Joe's house. As instructed he let himself in through the back gate. He got the right gate this time. Giving a hefty bang on the kitchen door to alert the old lady, he looked inside and found the shed key on its hook.

Ten minutes later he was hard at work on the Yamaha, boring his way down through the crusted gunge of oil and muck to the bike beneath. It was hard work. The last owner had done a thorough job on it, but he became absorbed in it. At first he tried working over the whole body work, then realised he was wasting time simply studying the works. That was educational but wasn't earning him anything.

Before he knew it, his watch showed twelve o'clock. The old lady suddenly appeared with a mug of tea and a sandwich. In the afternoon Tucker concentrated on one part of the bike trying to fight his way through to the original surface.

It was slow going. By the end of the afternoon he seemed to have cleaned about three square inches. At times only the thought of the £25 on the horizon kept him going.

But when he packed in that day, he stood back. The patch he'd cleared shone like a star in the light from the kitchen window, amid the grimy gloom of the rest of the bike. Suddenly he had a picture of how it would look when he'd finished. A surge of envy went through him.

He'd have to have a run on it when it was ready – just one. Joe wouldn't mind, would he? Joe would! Well, no need to upset Joe by telling him then. But suddenly the idea of riding the Yam became bigger in his mind than the £25 – well, as big.

As he packed the gear away and stowed the bike in the shed again, he found himself thinking about Yates, and wondering if he could borrow a spare helmet.

Day Thirty

Down to Joe's, open the gate, bang on the door, pick up the key, open the shed, wheel out the bike, get all the gear and get down to it. The cleaned up patch grew, but slowly. At lunch time he stood and looked at the machine as he drank his tea.

To his surprise, the old lady spoke.

'That's a filthy job. It'll take ages.'

Tucker grinned and shrugged. But she was right. At a rough guess it would take him about a fortnight, working every day. And that he was not going to do, for anyone. He'd have to get some help.

He packed in his cleaning in the early afternoon and rode home slowly. Stopping by the pub he wandered in. There was no sign of Trisha. An older woman at the bar made a face.

'She pleases herself when she comes. Wish I could. Expect she's down the college. All right for some.'

There was no answer to that. Tucker went home.

In the evening he rang Alan. But Alan got in first.

'Hey, Tucker, I was going to ring you.'

(What was he so cheerful about?)

'There was this bloke, got a six valve Yamaha, new for £350 . . .'

'So?'

'Was he lucky?'

'Well, yeah.'

'No he wasn't, the Old Bill nicked him for riding a saxaphone on the M1.'

'Alan, I'm killing myself.'

94

'Don't do that, yet, I've got news for you.'

'Is it good?'

'Sort of. Thursday night. There's a big disco at the college – tickets two quid with one free drink.'

'Where's the good news?'

'Susi is on the Committee.'

'So?'

'So, buy one, get one free – or two for the price of one for those who are a bit slow on the uptake.'

'So?'

'Well, I thought you might try that tasty one at the Labour – the chance to get close to her, instead of having that cruel counter between you.'

'I'll think about it.'

'Please yourself. Tommy's going with guess who?'

'Sure. Listen Alan, would you like to earn a couple of quid?'

'I can do that at home.'

'This is for a day's work not a week's.'

'Ha ha. If it's any scheme of yours, the answer is negative, Tucker, negative. Your ideas don't earn money, they cost money.'

'You'll be sorry. I shall ask Watson.'

'Well he's stupid enough, it's true. Listen, Tucker, you want two tickets or you don't?'

'I might well.'

Yes, he might.

Day Thirty-One

He gave himself a rest from scraping, wiping, sanding, shining, polishing and oiling and went down to the Job Centre. There was nothing doing.

On impulse he went to the Careers Office. Terry wasn't there but from Jill the secretary he got some pamphlets on self-employment, self-help groups and the like.

On the way back he drove past Roller's site. The gate was open and he turned in. As he rolled the bike down the ramp, he wished he hadn't. The law were there. The familiar blue car was parked outside the hut. Roller's group were standing to attention outside, Roller himself a little way apart, while the sergeant was busy talking, his finger pecking away at Roller's chest.

For a second Tucker was about to swing round and head for the road again, then he saw that the sergeant had finished his little sermon and was getting back into the car.

With a spurt of loose stones and dirt, the police car took off in a tight circle to head up the ramp. Tucker breathed again. Then the car stopped, its wing mirrors within an inch of his. The sergeant looked out.

'Are you with this lot?'

Tucker raised his vizor.

'I'm going down to run my bike round.'

'I should keep clear of them, if I were you.'

Then the uncle sound went from the sergeant's voice as he said, 'I've seen you before, haven't I?'

Tucker didn't answer.

'Yes, we have met. Can't think where. But it'll come back. Where's your licence?'

Tucker breathed out slowly. Keep calm.

He unbuttoned his jacket and pulled out his wallet.

The sergeant took no notice of the licence wallet.

'Yes, I remember. Outside the Labour, wasn't it? Handing out leaflets. That's it.'

The sergeant looked him over. Tucker drew in a deep breath again.

'Just watch it.'

The car pulled away. Tucker let his breath go and ran the bike down to the shed.

Roller nodded to him briefly, then carried on fiddling with the wires to the head phone set that hung from his arm.

Tucker looked at it. Roller said: 'He pulled the leads out. Said I wasn't listening. Listen. I did nothing but listen.'

Tucker nodded. Hughes burst in: 'Once you're in the pig van, it's no good talking.'

'What was all that?' asked Tucker.

'Searching – searching for number plates that don't match cars,' answered Roller. 'Said they'd had a tip off about re-spray jobs.'

'I think I know who did that,' said Tucker.

'Don't worry, friend, we know who did it,' said Roller. 'They just want to run us off. They don't want to do any spraying work themselves. They just want to run us off.'

'What did the law say?' asked Tucker.

'What could they say? We had all the papers. And we've got a lawyer, as well, at the Centre. But they warned us. Look. Two of our people are on probation. Do you think we'd be so stupid?' He paused. 'We have to keep in with the Law. But the others, friend. They'd better watch it.'

Day Thirty-Two

Round to Joe's, gate, kitchen door, key, shed, scrape, scour, sand, wipe, polish, shine. By lunch time a quarter of the job was done. He was not, but not going to get it done by the 13th.

That was going to be his unlucky day. Unless he could recruit some unskilled labour. He'd have to put the arm on Alan and Tommy tonight.

Late afternoon he packed in the job and went home, had a bath. Could he see himself doing this every day of his life? he wondered, getting yourself filthy, just to earn a living. There was a tear in his jeans. He had a feeling they wouldn't last much beyond this job. Ah well, that problem could wait. That problem was going to wait.

Feeling civilised again by early evening he drifted down to the pub. If Yates was there, he could take her to the disco after she finished her stint behind the bar, couldn't he? But Trisha wasn't around. The older woman was there pulling pints like a demon. Tucker decided not to ask her about Trish in case he got another mouthful. Instead, he drank up and headed for the college.

The students' union was packed, a small crowd on the floor and a bigger crowd round the bar. Tucker soon located Tommy, with the little blonde and established himself at a corner of the bar to survey the scene. He spotted Alan soon enough. He was hovering round a tight circle of students which seemed to have Susi in the middle of it. Humphreys was being squeezed out very politely.

Tucker shook his head and turned back to the bar. Another lad from school, now at college, joined them. They began to form a kind of old boy's club in their corner.

Tucker felt relaxed, drank, joked with Tommy and the girl.

'Michelle saw you – signing on last week,' she said suddenly.

'Oh yeah?' Who was Michelle? Then he realised – the tall dark one.

'He's only interested in the lady behind the counter at Box Six,' said Tommy.

'Oh, her!'

'Where's your mate tonight then?' Tucker asked the girl.

'Wouldn't come. She can't stand students.'

'Very intelligent,' said Tucker.

'Oh, I don't know, some of them aren't all that bad,' answered the girl.

'That's what MacMahon thinks,' Tommy nodded towards the group at the other end of the bar.

'Humphreys wants his head seeing to,' murmured Tucker. He looked round at some of the girls in the hall. He could learn to love students, if pushed. Tommy nudged him.

'Hey look.'

Four people had just arrived and were heading for the bar. He recognised Cathy Hargreaves from school, with a big fellow with a black jacket and frilled white shirt. Then he knew him – a Brookie he'd had a bundle with – many, many years ago. And behind them was Trisha Yates, with a someone. He must be a student. The four arrived at the bar simultaneously. There was a burst of greetings, jokes, exchange of news and the old school circle widened.

'Hello.'

Yates was standing just by him.

'Hello. What, no bar duty tonight?'

'No, got asked here, didn't I? Besides I need a rest from that job. They'd have you there all hours. And I need extra time at college.'

'I see, the pub works not good enough for us now?'

'Too right, it isn't. Believe me, it's hard work. Apart from the young blokes who throw up all over the place and the old blokes who try and feel your bum as if they're testing upholstery.'

'Like that, eh?'

He told her about the bike. 'I'll give you a run on it sometime,' he said casually, conveniently pushing questions of the law and licences into the back of his mind.

She didn't answer. The crush around the bar was growing. Alan and the student Trisha had come with, both squeezed out of the two main groups, stood and talked to one another. The crowd pressed Trisha against him. He nodded to the dance floor. She grinned.

'Why not?'

They danced. Yates moved well. Her eyes glinted. They laughed and shouted to one another above the music. They drifted back to the bar and she left him. As he rejoined the old boys and girls, he saw her with the other bloke and Alan. He turned to the bar, Cathy and her friend were next to him. They nodded. He was sure the bloke was weighing him up, trying to remember. He reminded him. There was a general laugh.

'Wonders never cease,' remarked Cathy.

'What wonders?'

'You and Trish. At school it was cat and dog.'

'We were just practising. Besides which, she's matured.'

'You haven't, I don't suppose.' She turned to her boy friend and launched into an anecdote which took them back to the second year at school. Tucker lost interest and looked along the bar. Trisha was standing talking to the other man. They seemed to be arguing.

Cathy nudged him.

'He's a nice boy. But he's a bit wet. No accounting for taste.'

He looked at her. Cathy ignored the look and went on talking.

He walked along the bar and stood next to them. He grinned at Trisha. Without a word she turned and walked on to the floor with him. Near them amid the dancers they saw Susi and Alan, turning and twisting glumly around each other.

Trisha put her face close to his and said: 'Somebody's having a nice miserable time.'

Tucker grimaced: 'I don't know why he bothers.'

She nodded: 'MacMahon can be a bit of a bitch.'

'Say that again.'

'But he's asking for it. He might have been Big Daddy at school, but now, she's grown out of him. The trouble is he hasn't grown up, has he?'

They went back to the bar.

'Why can't she just finish it, then?'

'Not easy, when somebody hangs about. I mean if you like them, but no more. And they cannot see it. Anyway,' she went on, 'I don't see why you have to tie yourself to one person. Why you can't have a good time with plenty of friends.'

'Depends what sort of good time,' he looked at her.

'Oh that — I don't mean that.' She returned his glance, then suddenly said, 'See you,' and she was gone.

Later he saw her dancing with the other bloke again. He danced with some of the students, but found now and then that he was looking round to see if he could spot her. Now she was at the bar, arguing with that bloke again. He turned back to his partner, but she was aware of his lack of attention. They parted at the bar and he found himself in the group with Tommy and the others. Alan joined them for a while and then vanished. There was no sign of Susi.

He looked at his watch. It was midnight. The bar was closing and the crowd in the hall thinning out. Tommy had disappeared now along with the blonde girl. He went into the gents. As he lined up he saw in the mirror the face of the other bloke further down. For a second their glances crossed then the other bloke looked away. Tucker went out and strolled to the exit. He felt relaxed, just a bit light headed, but not ready for home yet. What next?

Cathy and her boy friend stood on the steps outside together with Trisha. They turned as he came through the swing doors.

'We're getting a taxi, you want a lift?'

'O.K.' They stood close together as the taxi swung in to the kerb. As the four of them crowded into the back seat, he said to Trish. 'I thought you were with . . .?'

'I'm not with anyone.' She whispered, but the voice was fierce. 'Nobody books me for an evening if I want to talk to some old friends.'

She stopped suddenly and threw herself on to the seat. There was not much room for the four of them and as the door shut and Cathy's friend leaned forward to give the addresses to the driver, the other three leaned in and then back, to press together. Tucker pulled up his arm and laid it along the back of the seat and then her shoulder. The other two had gone into a kind of all-in wrestling hold further along the seat.

The taxi swung round a corner throwing the two more firmly together. Their faces touched. His mind was pleasantly hazy. He was just aware of the taxi slowing down, of people shouting, 'Good night,' doors slamming and the taxi picking up speed again.

They kissed. The taxi cornered again sending them sliding to and fro until Tucker had to support their combined weight. They leaned more comfortably into the angle of the seat.

When the taxi reached Tucker's road, the window behind the driver slid back.

'Anyone getting off here?'

There was no answer from the back. The driver shrugged and drove on.

Day Thirty-Three

Tucker was very late getting up, and very late getting down to the Employment Office.

But he felt ready for anything and anybody. First the lady at Box Six, then the Supervisor. After that the rest of the world.

As he joined the queue, the tall dark girl came past. Her eyes caught his for a moment. He looked at her, then looked away. Two could play that game.

As the queue moved up, he ran through his mind all the possible excuses for missing his signing on time. Then threw them all out as not being worthy of someone of his status.

He reached the counter. She looked up at him and smiled sweetly.

'You're not due to sign on today. You sign on next week and every fortnight.'

'But . . .'

'It's on your card. Next please.'

Day Thirty-Four

Tucker was broke again. He drew his £5 from the giro bank.

Round to Joe's place to find that Joe was away and so was the key. The bike was locked up and there was nothing he could do about it.

Back home to a moderate row with his mother. The bike

parts were out of his room again, dumped in a biscuit tin and left on the balcony. The trouble was that certain vital bits of Grace's bike he had brought home for more detailed treatment were mixed up with bits of his own. Spent a nice afternoon sorting them out.

Went round to Alan's and after an argument persuaded him to come to Joe's on Monday to give him a hand to finish off the bike.

It was not much of a conversation really.

'How much?'

'Two quid.'

'Get off, mate – four at least.'

'Three.'

'O.K.'

Then round to Tommy's for the same again. Except that Tommy wanted paying in advance.

'No way.'

'On the day then.'

'No can do. Look, I'll let you have it Thursday, no messing.'

Back home to find out that his brother had been round on a flying visit.

But no message for him.

Day Thirty-Five

Tucker dropped in at the caff on his way round to Joe's.

Trisha was sitting by the door.

'Hey, what are you doing here?'

'Meeting you. See you Sunday, you said.'

'Did I?'

He sat down opposite her. Raised his hand. She raised hers and pressed the palm against his.

'Can you remember anything else from Thursday?'
'Well, the important bits.'
'You were legless, Jenkins.'
'Not I. Head clear as a bell.'
Then he hesitated. 'What else did I say?'
'Come and see this bike. We'll go out for a run.'
His mouth fell open: 'Look. It's not ready, yet, and I've got to . . .'
She was laughing at him.
'Look, Tuesday, after you finish at the pub, right? We'll go right out.'
'O.K. It'd better be good.'
'You'll never forget it.'
'You could be right.'

Day Thirty-Six

A tough day for the team manager. Alan and Tommy came round to Joe's and worked on the bike with him. By lunch time Tommy had had enough. Only after some tough bargaining and the promise of another quid for the job was he persuaded to stay for the day.

They went at it flat out all afternoon until fading light stopped play.

The old lady switched on her light in the kitchen. Its beams shone out across the yard and picked out the bike now glittering in its red, silver and black trim.

Alan punched Tucker on the shoulder.

'Hey, it looks great.'

It did too. Tucker admitted modestly. All that was needed was to see how it ran.

And that he would see tomorrow.

105

Day Thirty-Seven

Tucker spent the morning going over every inch of Grace's bike, testing connections, bolts, polishing and touching up here and there. How many jobs like this would he have to do to buy a machine like this? He ran the engine. It fired like a rocket. In the end he became too impatient to wait and took the machine out on the road. Coasting along the side streets he could feel the power beneath him. Wait till this afternoon – and the open road. Better still a few miles of country lane really to feel how it handled in the twists and turns.

Just before two he parked at the pub and went inside. Trisha was at he bar, but she did not greet him. Face pale, she kept her eyes down to her work. As he came up to the bar she gestured towards a table in the corner. He sat down and waited.

Five minutes later she put a drink on the table before him and sat down. He stared. She looked desperate.

She looked at him a moment then without a word handed him a folded letter. He opened it. It was from the Social Security. Her money was cut off, just like that. She could appeal on form XYZ but for now, she'd had it.

'What's this supposed to mean?' he demanded.

'It's that twenty-one hour rule. I'm over the limit,' she said.

'But I thought you had all that worked out, even with this new graphics course.'

'So did I. It came to twenty hours. But they make it twenty-seven.'

'How can they?'

She bit her lip. 'You won't believe this. It's lunch hour and homework included.'

'You've got to be joking. That's sick.'

'They sent somebody round, asking questions – did I stay for lunch at college? – I do, once a week. Do I do home work? How many hours?'

'And you told them?'

Her voice rose: 'Why not? I thought they were checking up that I really was studying part time.'

'And they were really finding out if you were studying too much. How can you study too much?'

'Hey, don't shout.' People near them turned round. The older woman at the bar looked up, frowning.

'Listen. We've got to do something.'

'I'm going round there tomorrow to get the forms for an appeal. Trouble is I'm not getting much back-up at home. My Mum said 'Well, I always thought it was more trouble than it was worth'.'

Tucker jumped up. 'Listen, Trish. Get your gear.'

'What's this for?'

'It's two o clock,' he said. 'They'll be open after the lunch hour. We go round there now and catch the supervisor just as he sits down.'

'I'm not sure.'

'Come on,' he grabbed her arm. 'You hang about too much and they'll have your arm and leg off in this business.'

His urgency and anger fired hers again.

'I'll just be a minute.'

Five minutes later they were out at the bike. He handed her the spare helmet.

'I've told them I'll be back to help them clear up.'

'What did they say?'

'Not much. What'd you expect – them to give me a kiss?'

'Let's go.'

The doors of the Social Security place were barely open when they walked in, unbuckling their helmets.

The girl in reception looked startled as Trisha explained

quickly why they had come. She slowly shook her head.

'I don't think the supervisor can see you. He's got a fairly heavy afternoon. I can make an appointment for you on Friday.'

'Will you ask him, please?' insisted Trisha.

The girl left the desk and went through an inner doorway closing the door behind her.

She was back in two minutes.

'You're to fill in the form for an appeal. We'll find you one. If you need any help, come back tomorrow and one of our staff will help you.'

Tucker suddenly felt the inside of his head glow with anger. Taking Trisha by the arm, he pushed past the girl and barged in through the inner door.

A middle aged man was writing at a large desk by the window. He looked up in astonishment as they entered, Trisha turning to close the door.

'I thought . . .' he began.

Tucker took the letter from Trisha's hand and placed it squarely on the desk in front of the Supervisor. He looked at it, then at them, gave an inward sigh and said: 'Sit down please.'

He addressed himself to Trisha.

'As has been explained to you, Miss Yates, you may appeal.'

'But,' said Trisha, 'meanwhile, how do I go on with my course? And what do I manage on?'

'If your appeal is successful – and I must say 'if', then you will receive back pay for all the weeks you have missed.'

Tucker's patience, already under strain, now gave way.

'You've no right to do this,' he burst out.

The Supervisor looked at him carefully.

'May I ask what your interest is in this case? Are you a member of the family?'

For a moment Tucker was taken aback. Then he remembered.

'Anybody's entitled to bring a friend with them when they have an interview,' he answered.

'And you're a friend?'

Tucker sensed a touch of sarcasm in the question. Keep Calm!

'I'm saying you have no right to do this – spying on people. People are entitled to their dole money. It's not charity.'

'I'm aware of that. But as to our right, whatever you may think about what we do, we have authority.' He picked up a large bound volume from the side of his desk and opened it.

'The 1980 Supplementary Benefits Act says quite clearly about part time students in receipt of benefits – 'not more than twenty-one hours a week.'

He picked up another book. 'Everything we do is governed by regulations. We have to justify all our actions.' He looked at Tucker more sharply as he said it, then went on: 'It is public money, money paid in by your parents and Miss Yates's parent. While young people in full time education do not receive any benefits, we have to make sure that those on benefit as unemployed do not receive any unfair advantage.'

'Unfair advantage?' exploded Tucker. 'What advantage?'

Trisha intervened. 'You mean that if my family could afford it I could study as much as I liked, but because they can't you're stopping me.'

The supervisor turned to Trisha.

'If you were in full time study and your parents were in need, there are grants that they can apply for.'

'Yeah, and then your mob can come and spy on them as well,' said Tucker. 'If she told lies about her homework she'd have been all right, wouldn't she? Great.'

The Supervisor's face reddened: 'I don't think we can be deceived permanently by anybody's lies.'

'Yeah, what that means is, if you're a good liar you can fiddle social security as much as you like. If you're honest, you get nothing. It's a carve up.'

Tucker got to his feet: 'People like you sit behind your desk with your Acts and your Regulations, catching other people out. Life's a great giggle, isn't it? You're always in the right, they're always in the wrong. Then you go home to your wife and say – d'you know I caught half a dozen kids and old ladies fiddling their social security today. I expect I'll soon get promotion.'

Now Trisha was on her feet, her hand on Tucker's arm. The supervisor got up too. His face had gone pale, now. Tucker could see he was angry, but under control.

'I think this interview has gone as far as it usefully can,' he said to Trisha, ignoring Tucker. 'Please fill in your appeal form – if you wish to appeal. I cannot say any more.'

Tucker was about to, but Trisha took his arm and pulled him to the door. She did not let go of it until they were back on the pavement. Then she silently handed him back the spare helmet.

'I think I'll go home.' Her voice was very quiet.

'See you Thursday?' asked Tucker uncertainly.

She did not answer but walked away, head down.

Day Thirty-Eight

Down to Joe's. Get the bike out. It wouldn't start.

Tucker spent a couple of hours tinkering with the electrics until he located the fault. The engine fired with one kick.

Pity other problems couldn't be fixed just like that.

Last night he'd weighed up whether or not to phone Trisha. Then decided against it. What could he say? What would she say. He had his pride. So did she. And to be honest he'd made something of a cock-up of that trip to the Social Security. Just where it had gone wrong he could not say, because, again being honest, he couldn't think of anything he'd said that wasn't true. Perhaps he shouldn't have been so personal about the supervisor. But they had no idea what it was like on the other side of the desk, did they? None of them did.

He realised the engine was still running. The old lady was knocking on the kitchen window. He waved and switched of.

Best thing to do would be to wait till Thursday, then go down to the pub and have a word with Trisha. Give it all time to settle down. Think of the right thing to say. If he could.

Right now he'd concentrate on things he could sort out. This engine needed a good run. He'd go down to Roller's place and give it a ride round the paddock. That's what he'd do.

The big gate in the fence was open as he rode up. But the little grey truck was missing and there was no one outside the hut. But the hut door was open and . . .

What Tucker saw next made him send the bike roaring down the ramp to pull up just short of the workshop. Every window in the place was smashed. And that door was not just open, it was hanging off its hinges. Tools, spare tyres other gear were scattered around.

Letting the bike stand he went inside. The place had been wrecked. A vice had been ripped from a bench and hurled through the window. Someone had taken a sledge hammer and smashed up the bench, crunched up lamps and fittings into a great pile of chips and powder. The place was flooded with oil. He felt it suck at his boots as he stepped over the wreckage.

His foot struck something soft. He was about to toe it out of the way when he looked down. It was a body.

He dropped to his knees. It was Hughes. Someone had given him a bad going over. He was unconscious and blood still streamed from his face down on to his shirt.

As Tucker raised his head, Hughes' eyes opened.

'Tucker,' he grunted. He sat up, then held his head in sudden pain.

Tucker waved his arm round at the damage.

'Benson's outfit?'

Hughes nodded.

'How?'

'I was on my own. The others were out on the van picking a motor up. Roller's gone down to the garage . . . Hey, Roller!' Hughes struggled to his feet, then looked sick and leaned over Tucker's arm.

'Listen,' said Tucker, 'can you sit on the back of my machine? I'll take you to Casualty. Or shall I get an ambulance.'

'No man. It's Roller. He'll be coming back. They've gone looking for him. There were four of them. They'll kill him. They said they would.'

Tucker thought quickly: 'Which way will he come back?'

'Why, down the main road, then through the underpass and up Bulwell. Why?'

'I'll see if I can reach him first.'

'I'm coming with you.'

'Don't be stupid. I'll drop you at Casualty.'

The bike engine growled then took off up the slope like a racer. As they swung on to the main road, Tucker did what he'd wanted to do before now, let it out. Not that it needed much letting out. This must have a standing quarter of 12/13, no more. Funny he should be thinking about the bike at a time like this.

He saw Hughes into Casualty and shot away again, heading back for the main road. As he came on to it, the traffic was light. The lunch time build up had not begun. His eyes roved from side to side of the road. Where was Roller? Come to that, where were Booga Benson and his apes? What kind of car would they have? Why hadn't he asked Hughes?

As he turned into Bulwell he saw a police car, but it was going the other way. The road was almost empty. He opened out and thundered down the length. Old woman with shopping trolley, young woman with push chair, man walking along looking at form in the evening papers. No Roller.

Now he was back at the workshop site. The place was empty, wreckage still strewn about. Where was Roller? Had they got to him? He swung the bike round and headed for the main road.

As he came into Bulwell for the second time, someone nearly ran him off the road, a big beat up car with plates crusted over with dirt came at him from the wrong side. As it roared ahead down the road, he knew it was them. He gave chase. Then as both vehicles came up to the junction with the main road again, he saw Roller, down a side street, heading away, skating smoothly along the pavement, lost to the world. Tucker swung his machine and at that moment the car swivelled violently round. They had seen Roller, too.

Tucker was thinking and acting in one instant now, as he thundered past the skater on the pavement.

'Roller,' he yelled, 'look out.'

Roller glided on, one hand raising to adjust his headphones. He hadn't heard. Behind Tucker came the sudden bellow of the car engine. They seemed to be right on his rear wheel.

It was then he knew what the bike would do. He left them

113

standing, stormed to the end of the road, slowed, swung in a tight circle and came back, the iron pulsing beneath him like a race horse taking a jump. As he came up face to face with Roller, he saw in the same split second the faces of Benson's mob through the car windscreen.

A wave of his hand to Roller, and the skater swung crazily across the pavement to hit the wall. Tucker drove on, teeth clenched. Benson swerved aside and slid with a scream of brakes sideways across the road. There was a jarring crash as the car scraped a lamp post, then they had gone down the road as fast as they had come. Roller lay at the foot of the wall, quite still.

'Roller. Hey, Roller.'

Tucker bent over the figure on the pavement. The eyes were closed. Gently Tucker lifted the wires and headphones from his head. Faintly, then more strongly, the music came over. The full rich sound of an orchestra reached him.

Roller eyes opened: 'Would you mind, friend? I want the end of that tape.'

Tucker shook his head: 'You were nearly killed, mate.'

'True,' said Roller. 'Now if you will just help me up and point me in the right direction. I will get back.'

'I'll get an ambulance,' said Tucker.

'What for? There's something wrong with you, friend?'

Roller was on his feet now. He grinned at Tucker.

'But thanks. I saw them – heard them – coming up. I knew who they were. They've been up at our place, haven't they?'

Tucker nodded.

'Hughes?'

'Oh, he's O.K. I've taken him to Casualty.'

'Great. The others will be back there by now. I'll get there.'

Before Tucker could say any more, Roller was away, skates whirring down the road.

Tucker was about to follow, when he noticed something about his bike. How it had happened he could not say, but somewhere, somehow, he had picked up a long, jagged scratch in the paintwork on the tank.

He was just bending over the machine when he heard the soft squeal of brakes at his side. Without looking up, he knew who and what it was.

The sergeant spoke: 'Hello, now. Have we got a new bike then? Or is that somebody else's we've taken?'

Tucker looked at him. There were three of them in the car.

'Don't bother to answer now. You can think up your story on the way to the station.'

Tucker thought quickly.

'Are you charging me?'

The sergeant looked at the others in the car.

He shook his head at them. 'Educated youth. The wonder of our modern world.'

'No, laddie. We are requesting you to accompany us to the nearby nick to answer a few pertinent questions.'

He turned to the driver: 'Whistle up a waggon, Arthur. We'll have the bike brought in. Mustn't compound a felony or is it a misdemeanour, by asking him to ride it, must we?'

At the station, there were questions and then Tucker was placed in a back room. Phone calls were made. Tucker waited. Half an hour passed.

A fat, grey-faced constable brought him a mug of tea.

'They found that mate of yours – Kirman – on a job. He's coming round. You could be in luck.'

After another half hour, Tucker was called into the main office. Joe was there, standing next to the sergeant. He looked big enough to put his chin on the sergeant's head. He nodded to Tucker and looked round the office.

'Isn't Sergeant Harris here? I put his CH in for him last winter. Good bloke, Harris, runs a good ship.'

The sergeant stood back a little from Joe's chin.

'This young man says he had your permission to take this vehicle.'

Joe looked at Tucker again. His lips tightened slightly as if he were going to say something to him, then changed his mind. He turned to the sergeant.

'Yes, sergeant,' he said, with a touch of weariness in his voice. 'This young man, Peter Jenkins has been working on the bike in question getting it ready for me. He was to deliver the finished article today.'

He paused. 'So, I don't think it's a removing without the owner's consent.'

'Ah,' said the sergeant, responding to Joe as if to show he had a sense of humour, too. 'But wouldn't you say the vehicle was a little over the 125 limit for this young man's licence?'

Tucker saw the constable's shoulders shrug slightly.

'Yes,' said Joe, 'that would be naughty, if he were riding it. Was he riding it?' He addressed the question to the office. 'I had the impression he was standing by the machine, examining it. Perhaps he merely pushed the machine round.'

'Perhaps,' said the sergeant.

'Look,' said Joe. 'I think we've taken up enough of your valuable time, sergeant. I will take this young man with me and give him a good talking to, shall I. We don't want him to get into bad habits, do we?'

As they made their way to the pound at the back of the station where the bike was stored, Tucker thanked Joe.

Joe looked at him.

'Don't bother to thank me, Peter. I am just taking you out of sight of the station so that I can break your arm at leisure.'

'Hey,' said Tucker.

'You nearly threw that bike up the road, didn't you? You

worked on it for ten days, made a lovely job of it, then you messed it up didn't you?'

They stood by the bike and Joe ran his finger along the ragged edges of the gash in the paintwork.

'You are in luck, Peter, because I know a bloke who will touch this up for me tonight so that I can give it to Grace tomorrow as planned.' He paused. 'But you are out of luck, because he is going to charge me at least a ten for that, and I am going to charge you for it.'

He took the bike by the handlebars and wheeled it out of the pound.

'I'll give you the balance – whatever that is, tomorrow night – in the pub.'

That night, while Tucker was half watching television and half going over the dodgey state of his finances, his father came in.

'Oh yes, Peter. It's the 15th this week, isn't it? You and I have to have a word on Friday, don't we? Decisions . . . O.K.?'

'Oh, sure,' said Tucker, wishing he meant it.

Day Thirty-Nine

Tucker had a feeling it was going to be a trying evening and he was right.

As soon as he walked into the pub his eyes went to the bar. No Trisha. Not a sign. He braced himself and walked up to order a pint from the older woman.

Then he braced himself again and asked where Trisha was.

'Oh her. She's got the push, hasn't she? Can't say I'm

surprised. They put up with a lot round here, but she went over the odds.' She pulled on the pump.

'Came and went as she pleased. Thought more about that college than she thought of her work.' Tucker had a feeling he'd heard all this before, but kept listening.

'But what put the lid on was this week. A bloke came in and she went off – just like that, in the middle of lunch time, when we were busy. Says 'I'll be back to help you clear up'. Did she come back?'

She looked at Tucker as though he had the answer. He had.

'So the boss rang her and told her not to bother coming in again. Some people don't know when they're lucky. I'd be glad just to have the job in her position.'

Tucker had heard enough. He took his pint and walked away. He had, all things considered, made a Grade One cock up. He sat down. What to do? Should he go round there and have a word? Would that make matters worse? He took a drink. Maybe if he left things a while, that'd be better. Most of the trouble had come from doing things on the spur of the moment.

In fact the more he thought about the week, the more he came to the conclusion that if you wanted to stay out of trouble the best thing was to stay at home.

Better still, stay in bed. Maybe that was what the Russian geezer was up to. Maybe it wasn't a protest against the world, but just him staying out of trouble.

'You look like I feel.'

He looked up and grinned. Alan and Tommy stood there.

'Anything we can do?' asked Tommy. 'Like taking you out the back and shooting you?'

'Did I look like that?'

'You did. You looked like Humphreys has been looking these past few weeks. Same trouble? Gone too far and she's broken it off?'

'Watson, don't judge everyone by your own low standards. Tell you what,' said Tucker, 'You really want to cheer me up?'

'Yeah, why not?'

Tucker held his glass out.

'Go and fill this up for me.'

'See where your impetuosity gets you, Watson,' said Alan.

'You're wrong, mate, I was innoculated when I was a kid.' Tommy took the glasses and headed for the bar.

Alan looked at Tucker.

'Is there anything wrong, Tucker?' he asked sympathetically.

Tucker looked at him. 'As a matter of fact, there is. But as a matter of fact, I'm not telling you.'

'Be like that.'

As Tommy came back from the bar, Tucker noticed two men come through the swing doors. It was Paddy and Joe Kirman. They headed for the bar.

'Just a minute,' he said to Alan.

'Where are you going?'

'Won't be a sec.'

'The man's got a weak bladder,' said Tommy.

'Hello, Peter, my boy,' said Paddy. 'We were just talking about you. I was saying someone with your intelligence ought to be in university.'

'That's what my Dad says.'

'What do you say?'

'No thanks. I've nothing against college. I mean for other people. I – I want a job.'

'You say that now, Peter. What about in twenty years time when you've gone as far as you can and there's no future in it. If I'd had the chance, now.' Paddy turned to the bar to order.

Joe grinned. 'I can just see you at University, Paddy.

119

Professor Riordan, Chair of Demo-logy. You'd turn the bleeding place upside down.'

'And isn't that what it wants, the whole issue turning upside down, Joe.'

'You're right, without a doubt, Paddy, but as far as I'm concerned I'm just trying to keep my little bit of it right way up. And I reckon someone like Peter'd be better off getting into a trade, taking his City and Guilds. They still want you if you got the skills. But there's people with PhDs on the milk round these days.'

He turned to Tucker.

'Got the bike fixed up. He did it for seven. So you get eighteen. O.K.?'

Tucker breathed out. Joe dug into his pockets and came up with half a dozen banknotes.

'Here you are. Sorry to do that to you, Peter. But if you'd lunched that bike, I'd have had your guts for garters.'

'Fair enough,' said Tucker, pocketing his fee. 'Any other jobs you want doing. Let me know.'

Paddy grinned.

'He's got the style, hasn't he?'

He looked at Tucker.

'Can I buy you one, Peter?'

'No thanks. I'm with my mates.'

He wandered back to the table. Alan was on his own. Tommy had vanished. They sat in silence for a moment, each deep in thought or concentrating on drinking. Then the grinned at each other.

'Miserable pair of sods, aren't we? Why can't we be like Tommy, eh? Laugh a minute.'

'Excuse me, mate.'

They looked up. A biggish youth, their own age, stood by the table. 'I'm looking for a Watson, Tommy Watson.'

'Yeah?'

'I've got something for him. Promised it him a while back but haven't seen him.'

'He'll be back in a minute,' said Tucker, 'just gone round the corner.'

'O.K.' he said, moving away.

Alan suddenly looked at Tucker. Both sprang to their feet.

'I just worked out who that was. You know, the blonde.'

'Hey. No wonder he said he'd got something for Tommy. I bet he had. Come on, Alan.'

Leaving their half drunk pints, they headed for the gents, pushing through the now crowded bar as fast as they could.

'Let's hope we're in time. It could be a fate worse than death.'

Snatching open the outer door they rushed into the cold outer corridor.

'Tommy,' yelled Tucker.

He was flung back against the wall as someone blundered past them.

'Watch it mate,' said Alan. But the bloke had gone.

They pushed open the inner door. The gents was empty. Only Tommy stood there, pulling up his zip and choking with laughter.

'Watson, you are crazy. What are you laughing about? We thought you had been carved up.'

Tommy exploded again into laughter, then drew breath.

'I – was – standing – there,' he pointed to the urinal. 'I was right in the middle, when this bloke walks in and says – he's standing right behind me – 'Your name Watson?'

Tommy doubled up again, then went on.

'I nearly jumped out of my skin. Without thinking, I turned round – in the middle of it – and . . .'

Alan joined Tommy, his face lighting up in the first real laugh he'd had in weeks.

'The bloke got the full benefit.'

121

'He did, he did,' yelled Tommy.

'You are a sod, Watson, what are you?' demanded Tucker. 'Aren't you ashamed of yourself doing that to a father – if not a husband.'

'Father, what are you raving about?'

'That kid blondie had in the park, that day.'

'That was her sister's,' shouted Tommy. 'She looks after it for her. Gets . . .'

'No,' said Tucker, 'let me guess. She gets four quid a week'.

Tommy nodded. 'That's the story of our lives.'

'Speaking of life stories,' said Alan, backing Tucker slowly against the wall. 'While you were at the bar, I saw money change hands.'

'What money?' demanded Tucker.

'The money you got paid for that bike.'

'That's right, Jenkins,' said Tommy. 'So give.'

'All right. So that was three quid each, wasn't it.'

'No, it was not,' said Alan, looming over Tucker again. 'We negotiated an increase of 25 per cent across the board. And that means four each.'

'Right,' said Tucker. 'Well, you two buy the next rounds.'

Later that evening, when Tommy and Alan had gone, Tucker wandered over to the corner table where Paddy, Joe and their mates were sitting.

'Come on Peter, have one with us,' called Paddy.

Why not? he thought. He could see himself going back to school next week anyway. So, why not?

He sat down and listened to the conversation that noised around him. He couldn't quite make out what they were saying and didn't try very hard.

Someone leaned over his shoulder and put a pint in front of him. Then he heard his brother's voice say.

'There you are kid. We came up at 50 per cent.'
He felt notes being stuffed into his pocket.
He could count them tomorow.

Day Forty

Tucker woke late. His head was all furred up inside. His
eyes stuck together. But something told him he had to get
up. As he dressed, his mind went over the events of the
evening before. He could remember very little now except
for the final conversation when Joe, Paddy and his brother
had all given him advice about his future. It was all very
sound advice, if he could remember what it was and which
of them had given it to him.

What *was* clear in his mind was that he had a grand total
of £27 in his pocket. He would go down to the post office,
bank it and show Dad his account book that night. The way
he saw it he had met the conditions laid down. He had
earned money. He had paid his way. He'd earned his
freedom to have another go at the system, without going
back to school.

Right now he wanted a cup of coffee. Black coffee. Two
cups in fact. He wandered down to the caff, where the
bloke behind the counter greeted him: 'Your name
Jenkins?'

'Yes,' said Tucker warily.

'Young lady was in here just now. You only missed her
by five minutes. Gave me this for you.'

He handed over a letter. Tucker took it, together with his
coffee to a corner table and slowly opened it. He knew who
it was from.

'Dear Peter,

Sorry about this. I didn't want to talk. First the bad news. I got the push from the pub. I was so wound up and when we came out of the Social Security, that I forgot to go back. But I'll just have to look for another. Another pub a little way from here, where I don't know the customers.

Now the good news. I went back to the DHSS and they said I could sign on again as a new claim. I can carry on with my course. They're going to forget the homework bit. They say there are new regulations in the pipeline. Could be. Or it could be they don't want Jenkins smashing the place up. Who knows?

Now for the weather forecast. It was great seeing you again. But just a bit too exciting, if you know what I mean. One problem about you and me is something I've known since we were in the First Year. We're too alike – do first, think after. It's all right for both of us, but not two of a kind together.

'I'm sure we'll run into one another again, some time. Hope so. But a holiday will do us good.

You know what I mean,
            Love,
                Trish.

Tucker drank down his coffee, put the envelope in his pocket and stared into space. Trish was right. But that was the great thing about her. The very thing that caused the trouble was what made knowing her worth while.

Suddenly he remembered why he had to get up early. It was Friday. He was late for signing on. He staggered to his feet and walked out of the cafe.

At Box Six, the young lady slowly shook her head and silently indicated with her pencil the corridor where the Supervisor's office was. Tucker walked down there. A queue from the door stretched round the corner. He got to

124

the end, found a chair, picked up a 1950 number of Punch and began to read. Someone spoke in his ear.

'In trouble?'

He looked up. Seated right by him was the dark haired girl. She was grinning impudently.

Tucker threw the Punch back on the table.

'That's the story of our lives,' he said.

The Outsiders

'You know what a greaser is?' Bob asked. 'White trash with long hair.'

I felt the blood draining from my face. 'You know what a Soc is? White trash with Mustangs and madras.' And then, because I couldn't think of anything bad enough to call them, I spat at them.

Bob shook his head, smiling slowly. 'You could use a bath, greaser. And a good working over.'

The Soc caught my arm and twisted it behind my back, and shoved my face into the fountain. I fought, but the hand at the back of my neck was strong. I'm drowning, I thought, they've gone too far . . .

The Outsiders is an authentic and moving book written by a teenager about teenagers. It was published originally in America where it has already sold over 1,500,000 copies in paperback.

That Was Then This Is Now and *Rumble Fish* by S. E. Hinton are also in LIONS.

BREAKING TRAINING
Sandy Welch

Alison took the advertisement out of her bag and stuck it to her dressing table mirror. It was from the *Stage* and read: 'AUDITIONS: Female dancers and singers required. June 5th. Manchester.' You had to be over twenty-one, but that didn't matter, she looked much older. And she was pretty clever too, when she wanted to be; her idea about accompanying the school sports star, Tessa, to the race in Manchester was a good one, the ideal excuse. She shouldn't really have spent the money for her rail fare, but never mind, they could hitch up to Manchester easily enough . . .

Sandy Welch portrays in her stories the turbulent, frenetic and often bizarre world of teenage girls. She has captured their chatter and worries, foibles and obsessions with striking clarity and humour.

A SENSE OF SHAME
AND OTHER STORIES
Jan Needle

In this thought-provoking and sensitive collection of short stories, young people find themselves up against prejudice, hypocrisy and bewilderment. There's Lorraine and Mohammed who fall wildly in love, ever conscious of the family pressures which might force them apart; John feels trapped by his marriage and the birth of his son, neither of which he is emotionally ready for; Jim finds himself on trial for a violent crime after he accidentally becomes caught up in a demonstration, and Tony, who despises the mindless prejudice of his school-mates, is himself dealt a nasty blow by the people he seeks to defend.

Jan Needle observes with great compassion and sometimes humour the passion, despair and hopes of young people growing up in the urban life of the 1980's.

'Comfortless as his world largely is, it is authentic and convincing. The book deserves a wide readership, especially in schools: sensitively presented, it will provoke many adolescents to re-examine the clichés of both bigotry and tolerance.'   *British Book News*